Hard To Swallow

A Harriet Ward
Happy Trails Retirement Village
Mystery
Book 1

Glenn Rogers

ISBN 978-1-7324881-5-1

Published by

Simpson and Brook, Publishers
Abilene, Texas

Chapter 1

Nearly all seventy-five of us stood in the large multipurpose room in the main building of the Happy Trails Retirement Village and watched as the EMTs wheeled Walter's body out of the building. Marian and Judith were crying softly. The two young paramedics had tried to revive Walter. They'd even shocked him twice. It was hard to watch. But I suspect Walter was already gone by the time they'd arrived. Having been a surgical nurse for thirty years, I'd seen enough of the recently departed to know.

Stepping up beside me, Kathleen, a tall, beefy woman who loved to gossip, said, "Harriet, did you see what happened?"

"Yeah," I said. "We were about halfway though the first game. Walter was at the table in front of us and two seats over. Lilly was next to him. Louise had just called B-2 when Walter jerked and sat straight up, grabbed his chest, gasped, and then fell forward onto the table. Scared poor Lilly to death."

We had started bingo a little late because it was the 40th anniversary of Happy Trails, and the after-dinner celebration had gone on a little longer than scheduled. There had been cake and ice cream, and Cybil, the owner, had made a speech, thanking everyone for making Happy Trails such a wonderful place to live. Her father, Avery Greer, had built Happy Trails in 1979 on thirty acres on the south side of Abilene, Texas. As a kid, he'd loved Roy Rogers and Dale Evans, so he named the place Happy Trails.

After Cybil's speech, we began our Tuesday night bingo game, and ten minutes into the game Walter had his heart attack. Through the windows of the big multipurpose room, we watched the EMTs load Walter into the ambulance. Kathleen, still standing beside me, said, "Judith said he'd just had a physical and the doctor had given him a clean bill of health. He'd been bragging about it to his girlfriends. Why would he have a heart attack if the doctor said he was healthy?"

"I don't know," I said.

"You're a nurse," Kathleen said. "You're supposed to know these things."

"Well, what I do know is that doctors aren't God. They don't know everything. Besides, it depends on the kinds of tests the doctor did."

"Still," she said, "doesn't seem right."

"I agree. Walter was eighty. But if he was healthy, that kind of a catastrophic cardiac event seems unlikely. What did Judith tell you?"

"Just that he'd been to the doctor and was in good shape."

From behind us a voice said, "Okay, everyone."

We turned toward the voice. It was Linda Evans, the resident nurse.

"Given what's happened," she said, "I think it's best if we cancel bingo for tonight. Let's use the time to relax and think about Walter. Alice will have coffee and cookies available in the dining room in a few minutes."

"Big deal," Harry grumbled. "There's coffee and cookies in the dining room every night."

Harry's my husband of almost fifty years. Harry and Harriet. Cute, huh? Ward is our last name. Anyway, Harry was a cop here in Abilene for forty years, a detective for most of that time, and doesn't have a lot of patience with what he considers nonsense or foolishness.

"Don't be a grump," I whispered. "Walter was a friend. Let's go get some coffee and talk about what's happened."

"He died. That's what happened. What's there to talk about?"

We saw Ed, Jimmy, and Gwinn at a table. I sat down with them while Harry went to get some decaf and no sugar added cookies. Ed and Jimmy were both in their late seventies and had served together in Vietnam. After they got out of the army, they came to Abilene, opened E&J's Texas BBQ, and got married to their high school sweethearts. Over the years they did well for themselves, opening two additional locations in Abilene. Both their wives had passed away a few years back and they moved to Happy Trails. Gwinn had been a middle school teacher who never married and decided that living in a retirement community where she had nothing to maintain was better than having to keep up a home.

"You know," Jimmy said—he was a wiry little guy with lots of wavy gray hair—"Walter never had a bad thing to say about anyone. Always tried to say something positive."

Ed, a medium-sized guy whose head was as slick as a billiard ball, said, "You'd be positive, too, Jimmy, if you were as rich as Walter and had all the single women in the place chasing after you."

Gwinn, five foot tall and maybe a hundred pounds, said, "You're just jealous, Ed, because none of them are chasing you."

"Am not," Ed said. "I get plenty of female attention."

"And it's not nice to speak ill of the recently deceased," Gwinn added.

"How is what I said speaking ill of the dead?"

"You said his girlfriends were just after his money."

"I'd think that was speaking ill of the girlfriends rather than Walter," Ed said.

Gwinn frowned at him. "You shouldn't be doing that, either."

"How can you be sure he's dead?" Jimmy asked. "Maybe they revived him on the way to the hospital. You hear about that on TV all the time."

I said, "Doesn't happen all that often in real life, Jimmy."

"What do you think, Harry?" Ed asked, as Harry arrived with our coffee and cookies. "You think Walter was dead when they took him out?"

"Looked dead to me."

"Did he have any family?" Jimmy asked.

"Sure," Gwinn said. "You remember at Christmas time, his son and his family came to visit him."

5

"They had the teenage daughter," I said, "who was always unhappy about something and wore that awful dark eye makeup."

"Oh, yeah," Jimmy said, "I remember her." He took a bite of his cookie and a sip of his coffee. "I wonder how rich Walter was."

"Several million, I suspect," Ed said. "Why?"

"Well," Jimmy said, "on TV you always see somebody killing the rich old man to get their inheritance."

"Walter's family did not kill him," Gwinn said, "to get their inheritance."

"How do you know?" Jimmy said. "Whenever there's a murder, the police always look at the family members first, don't they, Harry?"

"Yes. But Walter wasn't murdered. He had a heart attack."

"Maybe they gave him something to cause the heart attack," Jimmy said.

I could see that Harry was trying to be patient.

"So, three months ago," Harry said, "when his family was here, they gave him something that caused a heart attack tonight?"

Jimmy looked as if he were trying to decide whether or not it was a trick question. Jimmy had not been the brains behind E&J Texas BBQ. He looked at me and said, "That possible?"

"I don't think so," I said. There was no need to tell him what I was really wondering.

Chapter 2

Across the room, several other women were at a big round table with Marian Goff and Judith Worth, comforting them no doubt, or trying to. Marian and Judith had been engaged in a friendly rivalry over Walter. And Walter, apparently, was interested in both of them, which was perplexing, because the two women were as different as could be. Marian, on the one hand, looked ten years younger than the seventy-eight she was, and was quiet and reserved. Judith, on the other hand, was anything but quiet and reserved, and she looked every bit and then some of her seventy-seven years. Too much time in the sun, too many cigarettes. And probably too much alcohol. What they had in common was an interest in Walter. One of them, they expected, would become the next Mrs. Walter Klough.

On the other side of the room sitting by herself was Martha Brentwood, a short, big busted, bossy woman who thought she was the cat's whiskers. Few people at Happy Trails liked her. Most everyone was nice to her because she was one of us, but I don't think she was on anyone's list of people you'd like to have lunch with. For a while she'd been one of the contenders for Walter's affections. Evidently Walter was a fan of very large breasts. But Martha being Martha had eliminated herself from the competition early on. There was something unkind, even ugly, about the way Martha was watching Marian and Judith as they mourned Walter's passing.

Harry went to refill our coffee cups and get us a couple more cookies. Given that they were supposed to be healthy, they weren't that bad—nothing some extra butter, spices, and nuts wouldn't fix. Sometimes life is about making do. Just as Harry arrived with a plate of four more cookies balanced on top of one of the coffee mugs, Lillian came and sat down next to me. I saw the look on Harry's face.

"Well, we need to go visit with Ben Johnson," Ed said. "Might go fishing Saturday if it's not too windy." He and Jimmy got up and left. Gwinn said she needed to go see how Elizabeth was doing and she left, too.

"What a shame about Walter," Lillian said, oblivious to the fact that half the table had just gotten up and left. "He never got to marry again."

"He was working on it, though," I said. "Wasn't he?"

"I feel sorry for Elizabeth."

"Elizabeth?"

"Fletcher. The tall redhead in 127, next to Betty and George. Walter had been cozying up to her. They'd been dating for several weeks."

"I didn't know that."

Harry was drinking his coffee and eating another cookie.

8

"Walter tried to be discreet," Lillian said. "Kept most of his dalliances off site, if you know what I mean. In fact, even before his Rose died, I think he'd begun seeing other women. She'd been sick a long time, if you remember. Couldn't meet his needs. The poor man was lonely. Over the years he became quite the playboy."

"I knew he'd been seeing Marian and Judith ..."

"That was just the tip of the ice berg. Walter tried to be discreet, of course. But you know how old women are— gab, gab, gab. Can't keep quiet for a moment. Partly, though, it was because Walter would have been quite a catch. Women after him all the time. He was loaded, you know. Millions. Now it will all go to his son. Of course, he's got problems of his own."

"I didn't know that."

"You bet. Allison Becker told me that when Walter's son and his family were here at Christmastime, she heard William, that's Walter's son, arguing with his wife Susan, over their daughter. Frances has got the same problem. Her granddaughter is pregnant and not married. And of course, Delores' daughter has three children, each by a different father, and she wasn't married to any of them. Can you imagine?"

"Well, I ..."

"But you know what I say, live and let live. Who am I to judge? After all, we did some pretty crazy things when we were young. Right?"

"Well, actually, I ..."

"Anyway," Lillian went on as if I hadn't spoken, "if Walter wanted to enjoy the ladies, who am I to criticize?"

There didn't seem to be any point in saying anything.

"That reminds me, did you hear about Charlie?"

I shook my head, and Harry got up and left.

"Bye, Harry," Lillian said. "Lovely man. You are so lucky, Harriet. Anyway, Charlie's been having trouble getting it up. Someone, I think it was Kramer, though maybe not. Anyway, whoever it was, someone said Charlie was having prostate problems. I think it's because he drinks too much. But either way, Evelyn sent him to the doctor to get some little blue pills. And evidently they worked. Ilene, who's got the apartment next to theirs, said the two of them were at it until two in the morning the other night. Poor Ilene had to take an extra nap the next day. Oh, and that reminds me, did you know that Cynthia is dating a man from Lone Star Retirement Home over on 27th?"

She actually stopped and waited for me to respond, so I said, "No."

Lillian took a sip of her coffee and was about to start again when Harry walked up and said, "Sorry to interrupt, but Cybil said she needed to see you."

"Okay, thanks. Sorry, Lillian. Gotta run."

Chapter 3

I was grateful for Harry giving me an excuse to leave.
Lillian is sweet, but, well, you see what she's like. The thing
is, she's extraordinarily generous. A couple of years ago, she
heard about a single mom whose car was stolen. The woman
had gotten laid off due to cutbacks at the company she
worked for and was having trouble finding another job. She
lost her apartment, and she and her daughter were living out
of her car. And one day while she was applying for a job, the
car was stolen. Fortunately, she'd left her little girl with a
friend. Well, Lillian heard about it and took out a loan to buy
the woman a nice little used car and rent her an apartment.
Lillian paid three months rent so the woman would have
time to find a job and get herself situated before rent came
due again. So even though Lillian can be a little tiresome,
she's a sweet lady.

Cybil's office is on the first floor of our large three-
story complex behind the information desk that sits at the
back of the large front common room. Normally there would
be ten or fifteen people in that front room, sitting on the

comfortable chairs and sofas that sit facing the large eighty-five inch flat screen TV that's on nearly all the time. But it was empty now because everyone was in the dining room talking about what had happened.

Cybil had stayed late because of the anniversary festivities. I knocked on her door, opened it, and stuck my head in.

"Harry said you were looking for me."

"Hi, Harriet. Come in."

Cybil looked stressed and tired. As I sat down, she said, "Shame about Walter. Any thoughts on what happened? I heard he'd just been given a clean bill of health."

The office that Cybil inherited from her father was paneled in real oak. The desk matched the paneling, and the thick, masculine furniture was a medium brown leather that provided a nice contrast to the lighter wood and the plush beige carpet. The office was big but not cavernous, and suggested wealth—old money.

"Me, too," I said. "And right now I don't know what to think."

"Losing any of our residents is always somewhat traumatic," Cybil said, "but this was so unexpected."

We were silent for a brief moment before Cybil said, "The reason I sent Harry to find you was that your insurance company denied your claim. I thought you might want to call them."

"For Harry's physical therapy after his knee replacement?"

She nodded. "Sorry. They said that since you used a physical therapist who came here, making a house call as it were, that it wasn't covered."

"Oh for Pete's sake. All right, I'll call them tomorrow." I stood and turned to leave, but stopped. "Are you going to call Walter's son?"

"No. I'll call his attorney. He'll call the family. That's the way Walter had it set up."

"Seems so odd to me," I said, "that Walter would have a heart attack like that."

"Does that sort of thing happen often after getting a clean bill of health from your doctor?" Cybil asked.

"It's certainly possible. The heart isn't meant to go on beating forever. Doctors can't see everything that's going on inside the body. But this one just doesn't feel right."

It was twenty to nine and most everybody had begun drifting up to their rooms on the second or third floors. A lot of them are in bed by nine or nine thirty. Of course they're also up at five or six in the morning. Since Harry and I are usually up until ten or later we're considered night owls. I took the stairs up to the second floor and found Harry in our small one bedroom apartment watching an *X-Files* rerun on TV.

I sat down in my recliner. It sat next to Harry's with a small table between them. "Did you know Walter was seeing Elizabeth Fletcher?" I asked.

Harry adjusted the volume on the TV down a bit and said, "Walter was seeing lots of women. I think he was trying to set a record."

"Why didn't you tell me?"

"You didn't ask."

"How would you like it if I didn't tell you stuff unless you asked?"

"I'd love it."

I narrowed my eyes at him. "You would not. You're a gossip hound, and you know it."

"No, I'm not. I just pretend to be interested for your sake."

"Uh-huh. Who else was Walter seeing?"

"Seeing or scoring?"

"You mean he was having sex with some of them?"

"Don't be naïve. He was having sex with all of them. Otherwise what would be the point?"

Harry was doing his cop face thing, and I couldn't tell if he was serious or just yanking my chain.

"Are you saying a man and a woman can't just be friends without sex coming into play?"

"Some can, maybe. Probably depends on the people involved. Evidently, Walter wasn't one of them."

"Uh-huh," I said. "How about you? Is sex all you're interested in?"

"It's in the top four," he said.

"The top four. So what are the other three?"

"The three Fs."

"And what are the three Fs?" I asked.

"Food, football, and fishing."

"So, sex, food, football, and fishing? In that order?"

He stood up and stepped over to my chair. He took my hands and pulled me to my feet so that we were facing each other. "For a lot of men," he said. "But for me, there's one other, right at the top of my list."

"And what's that?"

"Spending time holding hands with an old woman I met a long time ago." He kissed me and held it for a long moment. It was a good kiss. When he pulled back he looked into my eyes. The room felt awfully hot. Had someone adjusted the thermostat? I finally managed to say, "But sex is still part of it."

"You bet."

"But I'm a wrinkled old woman."

"Yeah," he said, his voice sounding husky. "But they're cute wrinkles and they're in all the right places."

Chapter 4

I woke up the next morning tired, thinking Walter's death had been no accident. My unconscious must have been wrestling with it through the night. I showered and put on a little makeup, which for me is mascara and lipstick. I keep my white hair cut short, so it only takes a minute with the dryer and a couple of swipes with the brush to put it in place. I dressed in gray slacks and a light blue cotton blouse. Harry was waiting patiently, watching Fox News until I was ready to go down to breakfast.

After a breakfast of scrambled eggs and sausage, Harry went to the pool for his morning swim. I normally try to walk while Harry is swimming, but I'm not fanatical about it. I decided to forego the walk because I had a problem to solve. I called the insurance company and explained in great detail why they needed to pay our claim. The nice young woman said she would resubmit the claim. Then I shifted gears and thought more about Walter's heart attack. Unexpected heart attacks happen. But was that what happened to Walter? The idea just didn't feel right to me.

There was no evidence that suggested anything but an unexpected heart attack, but I couldn't shake the feeling that something else was going on. The problem was I had no idea what. If what Harry had said was true, and there was no reason not to believe him, Walter was sleeping around. And some women find that a very unattractive behavior. What if one of them decided to get even with Walter for what she would have considered a betrayal? Martha certainly appeared to be angry enough to do something stupid. But what could she or anyone else have done to cause his heart attack? Agatha Christie was a big fan of poisons. Maybe someone was feeding Walter some form of poison that caused his heart attack.

I keep my nursing license current in case I need to go back to work, but that doesn't mean I'm current on all the pharmacological developments of recent years. I sat down at the computer in the corner of our living room and spent an hour trying to refamiliarize myself. Wow. Lots of new stuff. It was almost overwhelming. But then I realized that if I was right, I should be looking for something that would do what it did over a period of time. Something that would work slowly. It took me another hour, but I found something that looked like it might do the job. It was called menotega, also called teardrop oil, made from the pressing of genoa leaves. In very small amounts, used in conjunction with other substances, it was thought to ward off early onset dementia. But in larger amounts, given over time, it would build up in a person's system causing serious side effects, one of them being a severe cardiac event. It was oderless and tasteless, which meant it could be put in someone's drink or food. Was that what had happened to Walter?

Harry came back from his morning swim, and after he showered and dressed, sat down in his recliner.

"I don't think Walter's heart attack was a naturally occurring event," I said.

He looked at me. I sat down in my chair and swiveled it so I was facing him. "I think maybe Jimmy was right, and someone helped the process along."

"You think Walter's family killed him for the inheritance?"

"No. I think it might have been one of the women he was dating."

"And why do you think that?"

"Hell hath no fury like a woman scorned?"

Harry thought about it for a moment. "You really think one of the ladies here slipped a mickey in Walter's Metamucil not only to flush out his colon but to give him a heart attack?"

"When you say it like that," I said, "it sounds really silly. But Walter shouldn't have had a heart attack."

"You said yourself that stuff like this sometimes happens."

"I know. And it does. But I've also heard you say a hundred times that sometimes a good investigator has to follow his gut."

Harry raised his eyebrows and nodded. "I have said that. And it's true. So, are you saying your gut instinct is that something fishy is going on here?"

"Yes."

He nodded again. "I know the feeling. It gnaws at you. And I know better than to try to talk you out of it. Have you got anything to go on?"

I told him about my time on the internet and what I learned about menotega.

"Okay, so what you suspect may have happened is at least possible."

"Yes."

"Where would someone get some of this menotega?"

I took a deep breath. "I don't know. I just learned about it a little while ago."

Harry regarded me for a moment. "Okay," he said. "It's obvious that you feel very strongly about this. So you should stick with it. I'll help you any way I can. You need me to do something, just ask. Otherwise, go for it. Find out what you can about the drug and about Walter's last physical. See if there's anything there."

I got up and went to Harry and kissed him on top of his head. "You're my sweetie pie. Thank you."

"I love you, too," he said, as he stood. "I have a tee time at 10:45, so I'll see you later."

I sat back down in front of my computer and thought. Okay, if I were just the average person, not a doctor or researcher, and I was looking to buy a potentially deadly drug, where would I get it? A doctor I knew who retired about the same time I did, Kevin Goble, still lived in town. I called him.

After the requisite small talk between two old friends, I said, "I need some information."

"I'll help if I can."

I explained what had happened and my concern that someone had somehow given Walter something to cause his heart attack. "So what I'm wondering is, how or where would someone be able to get her hands on menotega?"

19

"Menotega?"

I told him what it was.

"And you really think someone got hold of some and used it to kill this guy?"

"It's a possibility I'm looking into."

There was a long pause on the other end of the connection. He was thinking.

"Well, I don't know anything about that specific drug, but generally speaking, you can get just about anything you want on the internet. Do a search for menotega."

"That's it? It's that simple?"

"It's not the world you and I grew up in."

I thanked Kevin, disconnected, and fixed myself a cup of coffee. Each apartment has a little kitchenette: sink, a cabinet, mini fridge, microwave, and enough counter space for a coffeemaker. Being a coffee connoisseur, Harry had bought one of those fancy coffee makers that makes just one cup of supposedly gourmet coffee at a time. It's good coffee. I don't know that it qualifies as gourmet or not, but cup in hand I sat down at the computer and googled menotega, shocked at what I found. All I needed to buy enough of the drug to kill someone was a credit card and a mailing address.

Okay, so it was possible. Someone could have given Walter the drug in several small doses that eventually caused the heart attack. Possible, yes, Harry would say. But what is the likelihood? And he'd be right. What was the likelihood that one of the ladies at Happy Trails was a murderer? Maybe I was getting carried away. Maybe Walter's heart attack was just a heart attack. I needed to know more about his last physical.

Chapter 5

It was getting close to noon when I went down to the first floor. Several people were making their way toward the dining room to stake out their table. One side of the cafeteria/dining room was floor to ceiling glass, looking out onto the garden terrace, a lovely patio with trees and flowers. On nice days like today, people liked to sit next to the window so they could enjoy the sunny scenery. In March, it was still a little too cool for most of us to eat outside, but in another month or two, depending on the kind of spring we were having, the tables outside would be full.

Harry would be on the nine-hole golf course with his buddies for least another half hour, so I had time to talk to Linda about Walter. Linda's office was next to Cybil's. It was not quite as posh, but was still way beyond what most nurses usually enjoyed … if they were lucky enough to have an office at all. Off her office was a large storage room where emergency medical equipment was stored along with the medications for our residents who needed help remembering to take their daily meds.

21

"Harriet," Linda said, "I can't share Walter's medical information with you ... or with anyone else for that matter. It's confidential. You know that."

"I do. But I figured since he's dead and I'm trying to figure out why, he wouldn't mind."

"He probably wouldn't," Linda said. "But since he can't give me permission to share his information with you, I can't."

"What about the idea that rules are made to be broken?"

"If we were playing Shanghai or Hand and foot," Linda said, "sure. But this is Federal law. If anyone found out, I could get into lots of trouble."

"Who's gonna find out?"

"Harriet, I can't."

I took a deep breath. "Fine. I guess I can't blame you for being a stickler for details."

Eyebrows raised, she said, "Stickler for details?"

Before I could reply, the door to her office opened and Kramer, one of our single residents, came in.

"Hi, Kramer," Linda said. "Nice of you to come right in without knocking."

"I heard voices."

"Sure you did," Linda said. "We've talked about this before, Kramer. You can't just open the door and walk in. You have to knock first."

"I'll see you later," I said to Linda.

As I stepped toward the door, Kramer said, "I'd like you to stay, Harriet, since you were a nurse and all."

I looked at Linda.

"Kramer," Linda said, "What do you need now?"

Kramer is our resident hypochondriac.

He turned his head slightly and pointed to a spot above his left ear. "Skin cancer," he said. "Stage four I suspect. How long have I got?"

Linda looked at the spot. I leaned in and studied the spot as well. "Kramer," Linda said, "That's not skin cancer. That's a liver spot. You're not going to die."

Uncertain, Kramer looked to me for confirmation. I showed him the back of my right hand. "I have them, too," I said. "You don't have skin cancer."

"You've been scratching at it, haven't you?" Linda said.

"It itches."

"Go see Rachel in the convenience store and tell her I said you need some hydrocortisone cream. Rub a little bit on the spot twice a day and the itchiness will go away."

Kramer left, happy that he wasn't going to die next week, and Linda said, "So why all the interest in Walter's physical?"

I explained what I was thinking.

"You really think Walter was murdered? That someone here killed him?"

"I know. On the surface it sounds ridiculous. That's why I want to know if Walter's physical included a stress test. If Walter's doctor did a stress test and everything looked good, then Walter shouldn't have had a heart attack. If there was no stress test, then it's possible he was on the verge of one, and the doctor didn't know."

Linda was frowning, trying to wrap her mind around my thought process. "Okay," she said guardedly. "I understand your reasoning, but I still can't discuss Walter's medical records with you. I can tell you, however, that Walter's son might have the information you're looking for."

"That's an excellent idea," I said. "Can you give me his phone number?"

"Sorry," she said, shaking her head. "Family contact information is confidential."

I found Elizabeth Fletcher, one of Walter's girlfriends, sitting by herself in the dining room at one of the small tables for two. The cup of coffee on the table in front of her looked untouched. "Hi, Elizabeth," I said. "Mind if I join you?"

"Please," she said, gesturing to the chair across from her.

I sat. "How you doing?"

"Fine," she said, struggling to control the tremor in her voice. Her eyes filled with tears.

I nodded. "I'm sorry."

She nodded and put a well-used tissue to her nose.

She took a moment to regain control. "I'll be okay."

"That's right. You will. May take a while, but you will be all right."

She nodded.

"I know it's not a good time, but I was wondering, do you have a phone number for Walter's son?"

She nodded again. "Yes."

"I need to ask him something. Would you be comfortable giving it to me?"

"Sure."

She picked up her phone, touched the screen a couple of times, and said, "I just texted it to you."

"Thanks. If you need to talk or anything, come see me."

As I was getting up, I saw Harry go by with his clubs, on his way up to our room. He'd be down in a couple of minutes. I went to get us a place in line for lunch. Lunch options were a flame broiled burger and fries, or a grilled chicken club sandwich with chips. Most of the Happy Trails residents are in pretty good shape and are active, and we expect normal food. None of this tofu and sprouts health food nonsense.

Harry and I try to have one meal a day at a small table for two, so we can talk to each other. The other two meals are at larger tables, so we can visit with friends. Today, lunch was our *just the two of us* meal, and we were still at our table for two when I called Walter's son. I thought it would be a cell number but it must have been land-line home phone because a woman answered.

"This is Harriet Ward at the Happy Trails Retirement Village. I was looking for William Klough."

"Hello, Mrs. Ward. This is Susan, Bill's wife."

"Hi, Susan. I think we met when you were here to visit Walter over Christmas."

"Yes, I remember you."

"Well, first, I just wanted to say how sorry I am for your loss."

"Thank you. It was quite a shock. We expected Walter to be around for a long time."

"So did we. In fact, that's why I'm calling. Walter's death was such a shock. Especially since Walter told several of us that his doctor had given him a clean bill of health."

"He told us the same thing."

"Yes, well, I was a surgical nurse for a long time and Walter having a catastrophic heart attack like that seems odd to me. I was wondering, did his last physical include a stress test?"

"I don't know. But that's a very good question. Maybe Bill knows."

"I hate to be a bother at a time like this, but I just think it would be good to know if the doctor missed something."

"I do, too. Can I get back to you?"

"Certainly, Dear." I gave her my cell number.

When I disconnected, Harry said, "You were wondering if the doctor missed something?"

"What? It was just an alternate way of describing my concern."

"Uh-huh."

"Beside, there was no need to upset her more than she already is."

"So you were just being tactful."

"That's it. I was being tactful. Thank you for noticing."

Chapter 6

It was Friday morning. We were getting ready to go to Walter's funeral when Susan knocked on our apartment door. I invited her in.

"I'm sorry I didn't get back to you sooner," she said, "but the past few days have been kind of hectic."

"I understand. No need to apologize."

"I talked to Bill, and he called Walter's doctor. And the doctor said the physical was very comprehensive and did include a stress test. Not that Walter was having symptoms that suggested the need for a stress test—chest pains or shortness of breath. He wasn't. The doctor just wanted to be thorough. Walter did well on the stress test. No sign of clogged arteries. So Bill asked why his dad had a heart attack, and the doctor said he didn't know. He said the reason men have heart attacks is almost always clogged arteries. Walter didn't seem to have clogged arteries, so he was at a loss to explain it."

I was nodding to myself.

"I'm sorry I couldn't be more helpful," Susan said.

27

"Oh, no," I said. "You've been very helpful."

"What do you think it means? Why'd Walter have a heart attack?"

"I don't know. But if he didn't have clogged arteries, then there must be some other explanation."

"What are the other possibilities?"

"I need to figure that out. When I know something, I'll let you know."

She looked across the room to where Harry, in his black suit, was sitting in his recliner. "Mr. Ward," she said, "I want to thank you for agreeing to be one of Walter's pallbearers."

"No need to thank me. It's an honor. Walter was a friend, and he'd do the same for me."

The thought of Harry needing pallbearers upset me. I didn't like to think of either one of us being alone. Knowing that it's eventually going to happen doesn't make it any easier or more pleasant to think about.

When it was time to go, Harry drove the Suburban around from the resident parking area on the south side of the building to the main entrance in the front, where I was waiting for him. On the way across town to the Eternal Slumber Funeral Home on Butternut, I called a retired cardiologist I used to work with. Victor Hugo. As it rang, Harry turned down the Willie Nelson CD he had playing in the stereo.

"Harriet who?" Victor said when he answered.

"Not Harriet Who," I said. "Harriet Ward." It was an old joke.

"Taking a break from your ceramics class?" he asked.

"On our way to a funeral."

28

"Sorry to hear it. Anyone I know?"

"Walter Klough."

"Don't remember the name."

"Never had any heart problems," I said, "until a heart attack killed him. So there's no reason you should."

"Happens that way sometimes."

"Yeah, but this one is strange."

"How so?"

"Walter had just had a very complete physical that included a stress test. The doctor said he had no heart problems. That he was in excellent health."

"How old?"

"Eighty."

"Hmm."

"If he didn't have clogged arteries," I said, "why'd he have a heart attack?"

After a brief pause, Victor said, "Was he having any symptoms that suggested there might be a problem?"

"No chest pains, no shortness of breath."

"Then why did the doctor do a stress test if there was nothing to indicate a problem?"

"Just trying to be thorough, I guess."

"Or trying to run up the bill with unnecessary tests."

"I hope not," I said.

"Me, too." Victor paused again for a brief moment, thinking. "While the main reason men have heart attacks is clogged arteries, you must remember that the human heart has a limited life span. It isn't meant to beat forever. Sometimes it just stops beating."

"I know that. But in this case, that explanation just doesn't feel right."

"I know what you mean, but I don't have anything else I can tell you. If there had been an autopsy, maybe they would have found something. But if the patient was eighty years old and the doctor said it was a heart attack, unless the family insisted on an autopsy, they're going to go with heart attack and bury the guy."

"Okay. I understand. Thanks."

"When are we going to play cards again. I gotta even up the score with Harry."

"In your dreams," Harry said.

"Uh-huh."

"I'll call you next week," I said.

Most everyone from Happy Trails who could be out and about was at the funeral. A few of the older residents had too many challenges to get out much. Martha could have been there but wasn't. Sore loser. It's a wonder she has any friends at all.

The minister, Pastor Oliver Trent, did a good job preaching Walter into heaven. I wondered, though, if the pastor was right. If what I heard about Walter was true, all the women he'd been having sex with ... What did God think of that? A couple of the other women I play cards with, Beverly and Mary, believed that if neither person was married then they were not cheating on anyone. What was wrong with a little physical pleasure? I had listened but hadn't said anything. Mostly because I wasn't sure what to think. I understood their argument, but I still had questions. I wondered what God thought about sex between two unmarried consenting adults. Still seemed to me like people who want to have sex ought to get married. Anyway, Walter was where he was, and I had nothing to say about it. I just thought it a bit presumptuous on the part of the minister to be doing God's job for him by putting Walter in heaven. Maybe he didn't know about Walter's numerous liaisons.

"Harry," I said, "if I die before you, are you going to do what Walter did?"

"Nope."

"Why not?"

"I think all the sex is what killed Walter."

Chapter 7

Alice Garvey, the Happy Trails cook—her formal job description refers to her as a nutritionist, but she calls herself a cook—prepared a nice post-funeral lunch for everyone. Walter's son, William, and his wife, Susan, and their daughter, Kimberly (still sullen and wearing too much dark eye makeup), sat at a table near the front of the room with Cybil and Linda. Those who had not expressed their condolences at the funeral home went by to speak to them.

Despite the fact that most of us in the room were in our eighties with a few in their nineties and knew our own time was approaching, the mood was light and the banter cheerful. There was no point in being gloomy about Walter's passing, and he would want people to be happy in their remembrances about him. So most of us sat around telling stories about the man we had known for so many years.

Martha was still conspicuously missing.

A lovely woman named Ellen, who was only seventy-eight, was sitting at the table with us. Ellen was thin and looked as if she were fragile. But she was resilient with a keen mind. Hector and Luna Rodriquez were also sitting with us. Before retiring Hector had owned a landscaping business that employed nearly thirty people, servicing several hundred accounts. Hector was in excellent health, but Luna was beginning to forget things. She also had Parkinson's. Their children wanted to take care of her, but Hector knew Luna would need more and more medical help as her illness progressed, so they came to Happy Trails where there would be medical help when Luna needed it. For the past few days Luna had been doing pretty well. Lloyd and Betty Mo rounded out our table. Lloyd had been a contractor. Some say he built half the buildings in Abilene. I suspect that's something of an exaggeration, but he did have a successful business. His hands were thick and strong, like Harry's, and his face had been leathered by years of hard work outdoors.

We had all been at Happy Trails long enough to remember when Walter and his wife, Rose, came to Happy Trails, so full of life, looking forward to their golden years. That was before Rose's cancer had been discovered. We spent a few minutes remembering them as a couple— Walter's love of old movies, Rose's tatting. We have several doilies that she tatted in our room.

"Didn't I hear," I said to Ellen, "that you knew Walter and Rose years ago?"

"Yes. We were neighbors. Walter and my husband, Kyle, were good friends. We'd go on vacations together. I remember one winter we went up to Denver to go skiing."

She smiled at a memory but didn't say anything.

"What?" I said. "Tell us."

"Well, the story is really about Rose more than Walter."

"That's okay. We all knew Rose, too."

Ellen smiled again. "Well, we were up at the top of a hill and were about to start down when Rose said she had to pee. She said she really had to go bad. She knew she wouldn't make it all the way down the hill, and of course there were no restrooms at the top of the slope. But she said she really had to go. So Walter told her to go over behind the trees and squat down and go. She didn't want to, but there didn't seem to be any other alternative. So she skied over into a stand of trees. And in a minute we heard her squeal and say *Nooooooo*. And she came barreling out of the stand of trees squatted down on her skis, her pants down around her ankles, her naked butt just inches off the ground, and down the slope she went faster than a bat out of you know where. So we all took off after her, but she had a big head start on us. About halfway down the hill, another skier had stopped to adjust his boots or something. I don't know. And just as he stood up, Rose goes screaming past him, and clipped him, knocking him off balance, and he skied off the side of the run into some trees."

"By the time we got to the bottom of the hill," Ellen said, "Rose had somehow been able to stop and had pulled her pants up. She said she didn't want to ski anymore and went to her room and stayed there until dinnertime. Well, Walter was able to coax her out to have dinner in the hotel restaurant, and during dinner she sort of loosened up about it, and we all had a good laugh. Then, after dinner, Rose and I went into the hotel gift shop to look around, and there was a man in there on crutches with a cast on his leg. And Rose says, *Oh my, You've had an accident.* And the man says, *You bet I did. I was on the slope this morning and had stopped to adjust my bindings. Just as I was turning to start back down the hill, this woman with her pants down around her ankles sitting down low on her skis comes screaming by and runs into me, forcing me over the side of the run into a stand of trees. I broke my leg.*"

We were all laughing so hard that people at other tables were watching us.

Ellen went on. "Rose turned three shades of red, and then all the color drained out of her face and she turned and ran out of the gift shop. The poor man looked at me and said, *I didn't mean to upset her.* So I said, Oh, please don't worry about Rose. She's like that sometimes. She has ADD and is a little autistic. She probably just remembered a phone call she needed to make."

We laughed some more, knowing that Rose had been absolutely mortified at what had happened.

"What did Walter say when she told him?" I asked.

"I don't know if she ever told him or not."

Chapter 8

It was a little after four, and Harry and I were in our apartment when I got a call from our granddaughter Nikki. Since her mother, Brenda, ended their sixteen-year marriage to our son, David, almost a year ago months ago, Nikki's been worried about him. David is our only child. We had tried for years to have children but couldn't. We adopted David when I was forty-four. He's thirty-eight now with a fourteen-year-old daughter. He's got a mild case of PTSD from his time in Iraq but is managing, working as a mechanic at the Ford dealership on South First. Nikki and David have always been close, and when Brenda left, Nikki chose to stay with her dad.

"His dreams are getting worse, Grandma. Sometimes he calls out in his sleep. And I can tell he's depressed. He gets up and goes to work, and sometimes he seems okay. But I know he's not, and I'm worried about him."

"I know you are, Sweetie. I am, too."

"What are we going to do?'

"I'll call David and tell him that you and I need some girl time, that we need to go shopping tomorrow. I'll suggest that he and Grandpa go shooting or something. Maybe they can talk."

Nikki liked that idea, and after we disconnected, I sat down next to Harry and told him about the call.

"Sure," Harry said. "We'll go over to the shooting range, then get a sandwich or something."

Our weekly ladies Hand and foot card game (and gabfest) was scheduled for three. Six tables for four players each were set up at one end of the large multipurpose room. As usual, at five to three I was the first one there. I hate being late. In a moment, Carol, Helen, and Marylou came in together. Betty came along seconds behind them.

"Lucile won't be joining us today," Carol said. "Says she has a terrible headache."

"I saw her just after lunch," Betty said. "She looked awful. Must be a doozy of a headache."

Once the game started we were pretty focused on what we were doing. Hand and Foot is fun, but it is also serious business. None of us enjoys losing. If a game is worth playing, it's worth winning. After several hands, though, we take a potty and refreshment break. While sipping some apple cinnamon tea, I asked Helen how Elizabeth was doing.

"She's devastated."

"Not easy to lose someone you love," Betty said. "When I lost my Chester it took me nearly two years before I was approaching normal again."

"Yeah," Marylou said, "but you'd been married for what, fifty years?"

37

"Fifty two," Betty said. "But how long you've been together isn't the point."

"What's the point?"

"How deeply you loved."

"Elizabeth and Walter had only been seeing each other a few months," Marylou said. "How deeply in love could she have been? Besides, everyone knows that Walter was just stringing them along to get sex. And they were willing participants. Mostly they were interested in his money. Visions of dollar signs dancing in their heads. If she's devastated, it's her own fault."

"That seems unnecessarily harsh," Betty said and turned away.

Marylou rolled her eyes.

"I don't think Elizabeth was interested in Walter's money," I said. "She had been very lonely. Having someone in her life again made her happy."

"What about Marian and Judith?" Marylou asked. "Walter was bonking them too, wasn't he? They shed a few tears over the old goat, but they're not going to pieces, are they? Elizabeth's just being a drama queen."

From behind us, Wilma, a wrinkled little woman with so many liver spots she looked like a Dalmatian, said, "Are we gonna play cards or slander the dead and dying all afternoon?"

Chapter 9

Saturday morning just after ten, Harry drove us to David's house. A couple of years ago, David bought a nice older home near the center of Abilene, not far from McMurry University. It sat in the middle of a big lot on a nice quiet street of older homes a couple of blocks east of Sayles between 14th and 7th, an area that had, for a few years, been undergoing something of a renewal. David spent six months renovating it, and it is now quite nice inside and out.

I got in the back seat with Nikki, and David sat in the front next to Harry for our ten-minute drive to the Mall of Abilene.

"How long?" Harry asked as Nikki and I got out of the car.

"Couple of hours," I said. "After lunch."

"One o'clock?" Harry asked.

Harry likes being precise.

"One should be okay."

Harry had said they'd go to Abilene Gun Range and shoot. As a retired police officer, Harry still carried his weapon, a Smith and Wesson 627 revolver, a .357 magnum. David also has a license to carry concealed, and carries a nine-millimeter Glock 19. I don't much care for guns myself, but Harry always said a gun was simply a tool for defending yourself. And he insisted that I learn about guns and how to shoot. So I did. And I'm a pretty good shot. Fortunately it's a skill I've never had to use.

I figured he and David would probably shoot a hundred rounds apiece and then go to What-A-Burger for lunch.

While the men did that, Nikki and I went shopping. She's easy to shop for because she looks good in whatever she's wearing. She's almost fifteen, but with her nice figure she looks older. She has shoulder-length brown hair, green eyes, and looks just like her mother. Fortunately, her looks are all she inherited from her mother. As a person, she's like her dad, which is a good thing. I bought her a couple of pairs of jeans, two tops, and a pair of sandals—the jeans in one store, the tops in another, and the sandals in yet another. Then we sat down to eat at the Chinese fast food place in the mall. It's okay for what it is: the same Americanized, completely unauthentic Chinese food you can get at several thousand other places across the country.

"So how can I help Dad?" Nikki asked as we ate.

"Men are difficult to help because they're different. They have this need for personal autonomy that gets in the way. It's a good thing and it's bad thing."

"I don't understand."

"Your dad, like all men, has a need to be independent, autonomous. He needs to deal with his problems himself. Asking for help is a hard thing for a man to do. They seem to think it suggests weakness. Male ego. So they limp along, struggling with problems on their own, usually refusing to face them, believing they can bury the problem deep enough so that it won't surface and get in the way of anything."

"But they can't," Nikki said.

"Not usually," I said.

"Why won't he talk to me about it?"

"I used to try to get Harry to talk to me about his job and the things that were bothering him. He told me that talking about it, whatever *it* was, was the last thing he wanted to do. He said that if he had a bad day or there was something upsetting going on, the last thing he wanted to do was think about it. If he thought about it or talked about it, he said, he just got upset all over again, and then it could take hours for him to calm down again. So he didn't want to think or talk about things. He wanted home to be a place of peace and calm and relaxation. Having a place he could relax and not think was the only way he could cope with all the stress of the job."

"But that doesn't make any sense," Nikki said. "He was just keeping everything bottled up inside."

"That's what it looks like ... from a woman's point of view. But over the years I've come to realize that despite what some feminists claim, there are some very significant differences between men and women, especially the way they think about and deal with problems."

"So you're saying there's nothing I can do to help him?"

"No. I'm saying that you need to help him in a way that he finds helpful, which may not be the way that you want to help him."

41

"I don't understand."

"If he doesn't want to talk, you need to let him not talk. Tell him you love him, that you are praying for him, and that if he wants to talk, you'll listen. And then let it alone. Share things with him that matter to you. Do things he enjoys doing. Find ways to be able to laugh with him."

"But don't ask him how he's doing, or about what's bothering him."

"Correct."

"This male-female stuff is hard."

"Yes, it is. But it's worth it."

She considered me for a moment, and a smile crept across her face. "You really love Grandpa, don't you?"

"He's my life. I love him more than I can say."

We dropped David and Nikki off, and as we turned the corner to go up to Sayles, I asked Harry how it had gone with David.

"Went okay. We talked. He says his PTSD is bothering him a little more than usual. Having bad dreams about Iraq more often than he had been in the past year or so."

"When did that start?" I asked.

"I asked him that. He had to think about it. When he did, he said they started getting worse a little while after Brenda left. He said he knew Nikki was worried about him. Figures she called you and that's what today was all about."

"Does he understand why Nikki is worried?"

"He does. Or at least he does now. I talked. He listened."

"What'd you tell him?"

"That if Nikki was worried about him he needed to be sensitive to her concern. That he couldn't expect her to just act like nothing was wrong. She loves him and is worried about him. I told him he needs to let her feel like she matters and that she's making a difference."

"You told him that?"

"Told him he needed to get some help. That he needed to get into therapy so he could work through the problem with someone who understood."

"You? Mr. *I don't want to talk about it?*"

"Ha, ha, ha. Don't start with me, woman. You know that talking to a licensed therapist about a potentially debilitating problem is not the same as just jabbering away about something to some old woman."

"Some old woman?"

"You know what I mean. I wasn't talking about you. You're not just some old woman."

"Uh-huh. And what did he say to this sage, male advice?"

"He said he knew I was right and that he would. But he also said that aside from the dreams getting worse, he was really unhappy in his job. He's tired of being a mechanic. Wants to do something else. Something that matters."

"He have any idea what that is?"

"I think he does, but he didn't want to talk about it yet."

"So you didn't press him about it."

"I did not. When he's ready to talk, he'll talk."

Chapter 10

I was concerned about Lucile and wanted to see how she was feeling. I went up to the third floor, number 302, and knocked and waited. In a moment she opened the door. Lucile is not fat, but she is a big woman. Over six foot tall and a little over two hundred pounds. She's fair skinned, has red hair, and green eyes. Must have some Viking genes in there somewhere. Normally she's happy and optimistic. When she opened the door she looked like death warmed over—pale, hallow eyes, slumped shoulders.

"How are you doing?" I asked.

"I feel like I been hit by a truck. Come on in. I just heated some water for tea."

"You sit down," I said. "I'll make the tea."

She dropped onto her big cushy sofa, and took a deep breath. The TV was on. She'd been watching some old movie. Looked like something from the forties. Probably a mystery. She used the remote to mute it.

I brought the tea and sat in a chair that sat at an angle next to the sofa. "Was it a migraine?" I asked.

"I don't know what it was. But it just about did me in."

"Ever had anything like this before?" I asked as she took a sip of her tea.

"Never."

"How long did it last?"

"Fortunately, not long."

"You gonna see a doctor?"

"You think I should?"

"Well, it certainly wasn't your standard headache."

"Maybe you're right. I'll think about it."

I sipped some of my tea. I'd learned a long time ago not to nag people about getting medical help. Encouragement was one thing, nagging was something else. Lucile would go see a doctor when she felt it was necessary.

"Other than your headache," I said, "How are you doing?"

She'd lost her husband to lung cancer not quite a year ago and she had a hard time functioning without him. He had doted on her and had done just about everything for her. When he died, she had to start doing things for herself. It wasn't easy. She'd sort of latched onto me. I didn't mind. Harry had always been so autonomous that he didn't need help with much of anything. And David, as he got older, had been just like him. It was actually kind of nice to have someone need my help.

"I'm okay," she said. "I still miss Sam." She had a far away look in her eyes. "But life goes on, and you learn to live the life you've got."

We chatted for a few more minutes while we finished our tea. I washed and dried the teacups and put everything

45

away. "Take it easy," I said. "Get your strength back. Your chair being empty during our Hand and Foot game didn't feel right."

As I was taking the stairs back down to the second floor, I got a phone call from Barbara Newman, an old friend. Barbara's husband, Troy, had had a stroke, and although he had "recovered" he wasn't a hundred percent. Barbara knew it, and as much as Troy hated to admit it, he knew it, too. Troy was eighty-four, Barbara was my age, eighty, and they were considering moving into a retirement community like Happy Trails.

"So I was wondering," Barbara said, "if we could come by and talk to you and Harry about it. Maybe you could show us around Happy Trails."

"Of course. We'd love to. When can you come by?"

"Well, I know it's kind of short notice, but could we come by tomorrow after church? Troy has refused to even consider it for so long, now that he has agreed to think about it, I don't want to wait."

"I understand. Tomorrow would be fine. We usually go out to lunch after church, but we'll be back here by one thirty."

"Would two o'clock be all right?"

"Two would be fine."

When I got back to our apartment, the TV was on but Harry wasn't watching it. He was reading one of his mysteries. You'd think that after forty years of being a detective he'd have had enough of mysteries. But he devours them like they were candy. Robert Parker is his favorite novelist. He likes the Spenser series.

I told him about Barbara's call. "Two is fine," he said. "But remember, I have a tee time at three."

"If they're still here at two forty-five," I said, "you can explain and excuse yourself. They'll understand."

"Okay. No problem."

"Ready for our afternoon walk?"

On the back of the Happy Trails property, next to the nine-hole golf course, is a lovely park with a one-mile walking trail meandering through it. There are lots of trees, shrubs, and wild flowers. In the middle is a small lake (or a big pond) with a bridge across it. There are colorful koi in it and a little fish pellet vending machine where you get a handful of pellets for a quarter so you can feed them. Strategically placed along the walking trail, about an eighth of a mile apart, are benches so you can stop and rest if you need to, or just sit and relax and enjoy nature.

As Harry and I walked, I said, "This whole thing would be easier if Walter had been autopsied."

"What do you think they would have found?"

"I don't know. Something, maybe. A drug of some kind. Something that triggered the heart attack."

"You still think one of the ladies here did him in?"

I took a deep breath and looked at the sky. A gentle breeze blew some small puffy clouds across the otherwise clear blue expanse. "Not really."

"But you feel that something about his death is hinky."

"Yes."

"Then keep digging."

"You know what I mean, don't you?" I said.

"Yep. Lots of cases I worked on involved things that just didn't feel right. There was something hinky about the situation."

"And you kept digging."

"I did."

"And sometimes it turned out that you were right."

"And sometimes it didn't" he said.

"You don't think I'm right about this."

"No, I don't."

"You think Walter's heart attack was a natural event."

"That's what the doctors think."

When we came to the bridge that stretched across the little lake, we turned onto it and walked to the middle. We stood there a few minutes in silence. Finally I said, "I just can't shake the feeling that something about his death is not right."

"Then like I said, keep digging."

"Problem is, I don't know where to dig at this point."

Harry put his hand on my back and kissed me on the cheek. I looked into his kind, brown eyes. "You'll come up with something," he said. "If I were a bad guy, I wouldn't want you on my tail."

Chapter 11

The sky was overcast and looked grumpy as we drove to church Sunday morning. You never know what the weather's going to do in West Texas in the springtime.

Happy Trails has three retired ministers from different churches who come in on a rotating basis and hold church services in our multipurpose room. On the few occasions we've visited, there were about forty people in attendance. A few others leave on Sunday morning to attend their own churches. Given that we have about seventy-five residents, forty attending a church service is a pretty good percentage. And those who don't particularly care for organized religion still have a pretty healthy respect for God. A religious lot we are.

But Harry and I have been members of our church for over forty years, and since we are still healthy and ambulatory, prefer to worship in our own church and visit our friends there. I'm not happy with our new preacher, however. He came about two years ago. He's still young, forty-one I think, and seems to be under the impression that telling cute stories is more important than teaching the Bible. It's not that what he says is wrong. It isn't. I just prefer to hear God's word rather than his.

After church we went with another couple, Alan and Sylvia Kincaid, to Cotton Patch for lunch. The Kincaids are younger than we are by a decade and are both still working. Sylvia sells real estate, and Alan is a political science professor at McMurry. He's as conservative as they come and communicates with his congressman on a regular basis. Needless to say, when we eat with the Kincaids, the discussion always comes around to politics. Which in and of itself is not a problem because Harry and I are pretty conservative and agree with most of what Alan says. It's just that sometimes I'd like to talk about something else.

We got back to Happy Trails at one thirty-five and were waiting for Barbara and Troy when they came through the front door. We went upstairs first, so they could see what a one bedroom couple's apartment looked like. The bedroom is big enough for a king-sized bed, nice sized bathroom with double vanity and sinks, a walk-in tub and separate shower, a small kitchenette, nice sized living room. Quite comfortable. Plenty of room for two people. Each apartment has parking for one car and a private storage room (a big closet, really) for whatever you want to store. We keep our Christmas decorations in ours.

We went back down to the first floor and started with the large front guest room. At least that's what Cybil calls it. Lots of cushy chairs and sofas and an eighty-five inch flat screen TV on the wall. From there we visited the large multipurpose room, the two smaller game rooms, the arts and crafts rooms, the gym, the pool and spa, the theater, the cafeteria, and the convenience store where you could buy snacks—chips, sodas, and microwave popcorn—and of course all the pharmaceutical necessities—Depends, Preparation H, Metamucil, and Poligrip.

The indoor tour took a little longer than I had expected because Troy wasn't as agile as he'd been before the stroke.

In the cafeteria/dining room, we sat down at a table, and Harry brought a tray with coffee and a dessert for each of us—apple and cherry pie. We sipped the coffee and tried the pie.

"You feel like seeing the outside amenities?" Harry asked Troy.

"Gonna need to rest a spell before I can venture out," Troy said. "But if the outside is as nice as the inside, I imagine I'll like it."

"It's very nice. Especially the golf course and the park," I said.

"Troy can't play golf anymore," Barbara said. "Could probably stroll around through the park, though."

"I could play golf if I wanted to," Troy grumbled. "Need a golf cart, but I can still swing a club."

"Of course you can," Barbara said. "Age is just a state of mind."

Troy looked at Harry. "How much?"

Harry told him how much per year for a couple.

"Cripes, that's a chunk of change."

"It is."

"Is it worth it?"

"It is for us," Harry said.

"Why?" Troy asked.

51

"Because it makes life a lot less complicated and easier. There's no maintenance—no lawn care, no cleaning …"

"No house work," I said. "No laundry, no dusting, no grocery shopping, no cooking."

"If you need medical help of any kind," Harry said, "help with medication, or any kind of physical therapy, it's available 24 hours a day. And if you don't, they don't bother you. Most of us here are still capable of living on our own. We just choose not to. Living here's like living in a hotel. You come and go as you please, do what you like. And if what you like is to do nothing, then that's what you do. If there are special dietary concerns, they've got that covered, as well."

"Why not just hire people to come in and do all that stuff for us at home?" Troy asked.

"You could," Harry said. "But it seems like you'd have to hire a lot of different people to do all that is done for you here, and you probably couldn't afford to hire full-time medical help."

Troy was frowning as he considered what Harry had said.

"And there are lots of very nice people here," I said. "And making friends and staying engaged is healthy."

Barbara was looking hopefully at Troy.

"Still a lot of money," he said.

"But we have lots of money," Barbara said softly.

"And I'd like to hang on to some of it."

Barbara took a breath. "Troy …"

"I know, I know."

"Speaking of lots to do here," Harry said, "I have a golf game at three, so I'm going to have to excuse myself. But I will leave you in the very capable hands of my lovely assistant."

Troy smiled and Harry left.

I waited just a moment while Troy was thinking. Then I said, "There's a waiting list to get in here. I don't know how long the wait is. But if you'd like, I can introduce you to Esther Meer, the assistant director. She can explain all that to you."

"I'd like to talk to her, Troy."

"Okay, let's go see her."

Chapter 12

Apparently Harry's golf game had not gone well and he was kind of grumpy. From what I was able to gather, Lyle, one of the regular foursome, was traveling and one of the other guys, Mike, invited a lady friend, Cindy, to play. Evidently, Cindy was quite good. Harry wouldn't say much beyond that. But he was not his usual post-golf happy self. Things smoothed out a little when we went down to dinner. Alice had fixed chicken and dumplings, which is one of Harry's favorites. We were sitting at a table with two other couples who enjoyed books and movies almost as much as Harry and I, and pretty soon, between the good food and the conversation, Harry seemed to have forgotten whatever had happened on the golf course.

While we were talking, Dan Black, our new resident liberal, came and sat down with us. "Did you hear what those idiots in Florida are doing now?"

"What idiots are those?" Harry asked.

"All of them. The whole state government. They're considering allowing teachers to carry guns into the classroom. Can you believe it? Stupidest thing I ever heard."

"Really," Harry said. "If that's the stupidest thing you ever heard, you must not have heard a very much."

"Somebody's gonna get killed," Dan said.

"I think that's the idea," Harry said. "Kill the bad guy before he can kill innocent teachers and students."

"Students are going to get killed when idiots start pulling their guns and shooting up the place."

Bill, one of the other guys at the table, said, "Why do you think teachers who are armed are idiots who are going to shoot the place up?"

"Because anyone who would carry a gun is an idiot."

Dan had only been at Happy Trails for a few months. People were trying hard to like him but he was making it difficult.

Harry looked at the two other men at the table and as if they had communicated telepathically, all three pulled their weapons and laid them on the table—Harry's Smith and Wesson, a Glock, and a Sig Sauer.

Dan, for a moment, was speechless. Finally he said, "Are those loaded?"

"Of course they're loaded," Harry said in a way that suggested the question wasn't well thought out. "An unloaded gun isn't good for anything."

"Do you know how dangerous that is? One of those could go off."

"No," Harry said. "They can't."

"Guns go off accidently all the time," Dan said.

"No, they don't. People who don't know how to handle guns fire them accidently and then say *I don't know what happened. It just went off.* But it didn't just go off. They fired it. This gun," Harry said, patting his revolver, "can lay here a hundred years, and all that will happen is that it will get dusty. It will not go off. It can't go off unless someone pulls the trigger."

"And the teachers," Bill said, "who decide to arm themselves will be trained and licensed and know how to use a gun. The only people who will get shot are the bad guys who show up to murder innocent children."

"Well, I still think it's a stupid idea. It's irresponsible. It's dangerous."

"Only for the bad guys," Harry said, putting his gun away.

"I can't believe I live in a place where people carry guns," Dan said as he got up to leave, mumbling to himself as he walked away.

The other women at the table just shook their heads.

Bill said, "What a moron."

I looked around for Lucile and didn't see her. On our way out of the cafeteria, I asked Sharon, one of Lucile's friends, about her. She hadn't come down for dinner.

"I'm going to go check on Lucile," I said to Harry. "Where will you be?"

"I don't know. I may go work on my painting for a bit."

"Okay. I'll find you."

I knocked on Lucile's door and waited. Nothing. I knocked again, a little harder. From within, I heard a weak "Come in."

Lucile's apartment was one of the smaller one-room units. The bed was against the far wall. Lucile lay on it, hands to the side of her head, groaning, obviously in serious pain. I checked her pulse. Slightly elevated, but nothing to be worried about. I put my hand on her head. She wasn't running a fever. I called Linda Evans. "You need to come up to Lucile's room."

"What's wrong?"

"Serious head pain. Pulse and temp are normal."

"Okay. Be right there."

"How long have you been hurting?"

Instead of answering, she rolled onto her side and vomited. I was cleaning it up when Linda arrived. The pain appeared to be getting worse. Linda took Lucile's blood pressure. It was slightly elevated. She gave her a shot to help the pain. In a few minutes the shot began working and Lucile began to relax. After a couple more minutes Lucile apologized for vomiting.

"Don't worry about," I said.

"Please tell me this is the first one of these you've had," Linda said.

Lucile shook her head. "This is the third one."

"Why didn't you come to me after the first one?"

"I thought it was just a bad headache. You don't see a nurse because you have a headache. But the pain is getting worse."

"You need to see a doctor."

Linda was talking about Dr. Lawrence Bascom, the gerontologist who takes care of most of us at Happy Trails. Linda went to the other side of the room and called him. He would take calls from Linda any time, and tell her how to proceed.

"Okay," Linda said, coming back over to us. "Dr. Bascom wants to see you first thing in the morning. He'll schedule an MRI if there's an open spot. The shot I gave you will help you sleep. If you have any additional pain during the night, call Greg, the duty nurse. I'll explain to him what's going on. And I'll be here in the morning to take you to see Dr. Bascom."

"I'd like Harriet to come along," Lucile said.

Linda looked at me.

"I'd be glad to come along," I said. "What time?"

"We should leave about seven forty-five."

"We'll be ready."

The pain had exhausted Lucile, so I helped get her undressed and into bed. She was asleep before I was out of her room. I left the door unlocked just in case we needed to get back in.

Harry was in the art room alone working on his landscape, which was coming along nicely, I thought. We'd gone out to the ruins at Fort Phantom late one afternoon and taken several pictures of what was left of the old fort at sunset. There was one especially good photo that Harry was turning into an equally good painting. He was working to get the pinkish-orange sky just right. I liked it.

"Lucile okay?" he asked as he gently added color to the canvas.

"She had another doozy of a headache. She vomited. Linda gave her a shot, so she's asleep right now, but something's not right."

Harry looked at me. "Serious?"

"Probably. Bascom will get her in for an MRI in the morning. She asked if I would go with her, and I said I would. I hope that's okay."

"Of course, it's okay. You know that. If you can make a difference for her, you should."

I kissed him on the cheek. "Thank you. You're a sweetie."

"I know. But don't tell anyone else. I have an image to maintain."

"Your secret is safe with me. Now how about we stroll down the lane to the ice cream parlor?"

"Does that mean they got the soft-serve machine in the dining room fixed?"

"It does."

"Then we should go."

Chapter 13

I'd gotten up early and had gone up to Lucile's room to be sure she was up and ready to go. We had time to go to the cafeteria for some yogurt and a cup of coffee, and were waiting at the front entrance when Linda pulled her car around. I really appreciated Linda. She wasn't just a nurse who did her job. She cared about the people at Happy Trails and quite often worked long hours to be sure everyone's needs were being met.

The hospital where Dr. Bascom had his office, near Abilene Regional Medical, was only ten minutes away. Linda let Lucile and me off at the entrance and went to park the car while Lucile checked in. It was eight o'clock on the dot. In a couple of minutes, the nurse called Lucile's name. Linda was just coming in the door and all three of us went back.

Dr. Lawrence Bascom is tall and lean with a lot of unruly brown wavy hair. And he was movie star handsome. I suspected some of the ladies at Happy Trails sometimes feigned illness just to have him examine them. He asked

Lucile to explain what had happened. She told him about the terrible pain in her head and the vomiting. Dr. Bascom listened patiently, asked a few questions, and looked into her eyes with his ophthalmoscope. He took her blood pressure and listened to her heart and lungs.

"Okay," he said. "I've got you scheduled for an MRI. Linda can take you over there. When you're done, you can go home. They'll get the MRI to me, and I'll call and let you know what going on in there. Just try to relax, okay?"

Lucile was worried. I felt sorry for her. As soon as we got checked in at the MRI desk, the technician came out and took Lucile back. "It'll be about an hour," the young man said.

Linda and I settled in to wait, Linda thumbing through a magazine while I took a Janet Evanovich paperback out of my purse. I tried to read but was too distracted. I closed the book and put it away.

Linda looked at me. "Lucile or Walter?" she asked.

"Is it that apparent?"

"Probably only to someone who knows you."

"I'm worried about Lucile, of course, but I can't get Walter's death out of my head."

"Were you able to get the information you were asking me about?"

"Yes."

"And?"

"His physical included a stress test," I said. "His arteries weren't clogged. His heart was getting plenty of blood. He shouldn't have had a heart attack."

"But he did."

"Yes."

"And you can't let it go."

"No."

"Wish I could help you."

"Was he taking anything new?" I asked.

"Not that I know of." She considered me for a moment. "You really think he might have been taking something that generated the attack?"

"I don't know. I'm just trying to come up with something that makes sense to me. There are all sorts of medications that can have adverse effects on the heart."

"I suppose it's possible," Linda said. "It's unlikely, though, I think. Walter had no reason to be taking additional medications of any kind. For as old as he was, he was as healthy as a horse."

"Which is exactly why his heart attack makes no sense," I said.

"I agree. And I wish I could explain it, but I can't."

No point in beating a dead horse, so Linda went back to her magazine and I tried reading again, but the cause of Walter's heart attack was like an itch in the back of my brain. I put the book away again and used my phone to look up medications where heart problems might be side effects.

I was still reading when Lucile came out, looking tired and stressed.

Chapter 14

We were on our way back to Happy Trails, only a hundred yards or so from the front entrance, when Lucile screamed from the backseat. When I turned in the seat, Lucile had her hands to the sides of her head, her eyes large and terrified. As Linda pulled to the side of the road, Lucile's eyes rolled back into her head and she slumped in the seat. I got out, ripped open the back door and climbed in. Linda reached in through the other back door. I felt for a pulse in Lucile's neck and couldn't find one.

"Get us to an ER," I said to Linda as I pulled Lucile around so she was lying flat on the seat. As Linda got back in the driver's seat, I started chest compressions.

Linda headed up Catclaw to Southwest, turned right and went up to Clack and turned again, headed for the ER that was a little further up on Clack. I kept up the chest compressions all the way to the ER. Linda jumped out and ran inside, and in a few seconds two emergency nurses came out, emergency equipment in their hands. I moved out so they could take over, but it was too late. Lucile was gone.

I looked at Linda. She was as shocked as I was. What had happened? One minute Lucile had been talking about being in the MRI machine and the next she was gone. As a surgical nurse for thirty plus years, I'd seen people die on the table. It was always sad. But those people had been patients. Lucile was a friend. It was different. First Walter, now Lucile. What was going on? Was there a connection? How could there be? Walter had a heart attack. Whatever had killed Lucile wasn't a heart attack.

They brought a gurney out and wheeled Lucile's body inside and took her in back. Linda and I went in and gave them some basic information. They wanted to know her next of kin. Neither of us knew. Cybil would have to provide additional details. They said they would wait for Cybil to call.

Linda and I rode in silence back to Happy Trails and went straight to Cybil's office.

"Dead?" Cybil said, hand to heart. "What happened?"

I explained.

"Does Lawrence know?"

"No."

Cybil punched in his number and put the phone on speaker.

When Dr. Bascom answered he said, "Hi, Cybil. If you're calling about Lucile, I haven't had time to look at the MRI yet."

"Lawrence," Linda said.

"Linda," he said.

"Lucile died on the way back here. She's dead."

There was a moment of silence. Then, "What happened?"

Linda explained.

64

"I know she was a friend," he said. "I'm sorry. I need some time to study the MRI. I'll call you back in a little while."

We sat there a moment, stunned by what had happened. Finally, I said, "The folks at the ER, the one down there on Clack, need some information."

"Okay," Cybil said, "I'll call them."

"Does she have family in the area?"

"No. There is a sister-in-law back east somewhere. I'll need to check the file."

"We should tell everyone at lunchtime," Linda said.

"Maybe Dr. Bascom will have called by then," I said, "and we'll have something by way of an explanation."

"That would make things simpler," Cybil said. "This is going to be very upsetting, coming so close on the heels of Walter's passing."

"Speaking of which," I said, "does it bother you that another resident has died in such an unexpected manner?"

Cybil looked confused. "Well, it's certainly an odd coincidence."

"You think it's just coincidence?" I said.

"What else could it be?"

"I don't know. But to simply write it off to coincidence seems something of a stretch to me."

"Are you suggesting that something sinister is going on?"

I took a deep breath. I didn't want to get myself in too deep or come off sounding like a conspiracy theory nut case. "I don't know. I just know that neither of them appeared to have any health problems, and now within a matter of days, they're both dead."

Chapter 15

"Dead!" Harry said. "What happened?"

I explained the whole thing to him in excruciating detail. It took longer to tell because I was crying. Harry got up from his chair as I was telling the story and hugged me.

"Aw, Sweetie, I'm sorry," he said when I finished. "I know she was a friend. Makes it a lot harder."

I buried my face in his chest and cried for a couple of minutes while he held me and patted my back. Then I caught my breath and stepped back. "I'm sorry," I said. "I got your shirt all wet and snotty."

"Doesn't matter. You okay?"

I took another deep breath and nodded. I sat down. "It just sort of all hit at once, I guess. First Walter, then Lucile."

"I imagine the way it happened had something to do with it as well."

He was right. It had.

"Do you have any idea what caused it?" he asked.

"If I had to guess, I'd say a brain tumor. We'll know more when Dr. Bascom has had time to look at the MRI."

Harry made tea, and we both sat quietly and drank it. After twenty minutes or so, I felt better. "I need to go talk to Linda. See if Dr. Bascom has gotten back to her yet."

"Okay. I'm going down to the pool to swim. You want to eat lunch here or go out somewhere else. Get away from it all for a little while?"

"No, I'd rather stay here. Some of Lucile's friends may need to talk."

I went to Linda's office.

"You hear from Dr. Bascom yet?"

"Just got off the phone with him," she said. "The MRI showed that Lucile had a brain tumor. A GBM. Good-sized and probably fast growing since the pain got so severe so quickly."

That made sense.

"Did he have any thoughts on what caused it?"

"I was just looking that up. Mostly they're generated by inherited genetic deficiencies."

"So her ancestors killed her," I said. I knew I sound snarky but I didn't care. It wasn't a good answer. A friend had died in my hands, and telling me her DNA did it wasn't making any sense to me.

"I'm sorry," Linda said softly.

"I know," I said. "Me, too."

Emotion was welling up in me again, but I was determined not to let the dam break. "Have you told Cybil?"

"Not yet. I was just getting ready to. Want to come with me?"

"No. You go ahead. I need to think."

A cold front had blown in, and it was chilly out. March in West Texas can be that way—wonderfully warm or downright wintry. The temperature was 54° but the wind chill made it feel colder, so I grabbed a jacket. I made sure I had a couple of quarters so I could feed the fish, and headed out to the park where I could be alone and think.

The koi were glad to see me, and the dozen or more who came to be fed created a colorful collage in the water. As I dropped the pellets into the water, creating something of a feeding frenzy, I wondered if the koi felt the loss of another fish. Probably not. No limbic system. Dogs mourn, though. They have a limbic system like we do. I cried some more. I'd felt so sorry for Lucile. She'd been so lost after Sam died. Like I would be without Harry. Maybe Sam and Lucile are together again. Be nice if it worked that way. I don't know if it does or not. Lots of people think so, but there's no way to know how things work in the afterlife. Just wanting it to be so doesn't make it so. Sam died because he had lung cancer. He had lung cancer because he smoked for forty years. It was his own fault. Why did Lucile die? She didn't do anything to cause this … Or did she? Was her brain tumor the result of a genetic crapshoot, or did she do something to cause it? Did Walter do something to cause his heart attack? I didn't know, but I wanted to.

The koi would have kept eating as long as I kept feeding them, but I'd fed them enough. Besides, I was getting cold. It was eleven thirty. Getting on toward lunchtime. Time to find Harry so we could eat lunch.

Though our cook, Alice, usually tried to accommodate our nutritional preferences, which tended toward meat and potatoes, she was occasionally overcome by a desire to feed us healthy food. Today was one of those days. Prominent along the buffet table was grilled chicken, which was fine, but the chicken was accompanied by a generous offering of different kinds of steamed vegetables, including broccoli, which meant Millie was going to be very happy. The woman loved vegetables, but her favorite was broccoli. The problem was that broccoli doesn't love her. Millie suffered from an inability to digest vegetables. Instead of being lactose intolerant, she was fiber intolerant. The poor woman could clear out a room faster than if someone pulled the fire alarm. Additionally, Millie seemed blissfully unaware of the problem.

Millie was three ahead of us in the line. We watched where she sat, and like several other people, sat as far away from her as we could. Harry had gotten green beans and carrots to go with his chicken breast. I had built myself a nice salad at the salad bar. We were about half way through lunch when Cybil stood and asked for everyone's attention. Wisely, she kept her announcement brief.

"I'm deeply sorry to have to tell you that this morning at nine thirty, on the way back from a doctor's appointment, Lucile suddenly and unexpectedly passed away."

There was a collective gasp.

"Her death," Cybil said, "was the result of a very fast-growing brain tumor. Harriet and Linda were with her when she passed."

Cybil sat back down. The room was very quiet for several seconds before soft conversation began again at each of the tables. Mildred Pickle, who was sitting at the table next to us moved to an empty chair next to me. Mildred was a chunky woman with several chins and a headful of unruly gray curls. "Did she suffer?" Mildred asked.

"The pain was intense, but brief," I said. "She was gone quickly."

"Well, that's something anyway. Better than lingering like her Sam did."

I had to agree.

"You okay?" she asked me.

"Yeah, I'm fine."

"Was she on HRT?" Mildred asked.

"I don't know."

"If she was, the HRT could have caused the tumor. My sister has a friend who was on HRT and developed a brain tumor. Neurosurgeon told her it was probably the HRT that caused it."

Now that Mildred had said it, I remembered hearing that one of the possible side effects of HRT was brain tumors.

"Wouldn't catch me taking that stuff," Mildred said. "Better to dry up and grow a mustache than to take the stuff and end up with a brain tumor."

"I really don't know whether Lucile was on HRT or not," I said.

But I intended to find out.

Chapter 16

News of Lucile's death brought a shadow of gloom with it that hung over Happy Trails throughout the afternoon. People appeared to be busy, trying to distract themselves, but the normal level of energy was way down. I went to my ceramics class, but just couldn't get the creative juices flowing. I put the urn I was trying to paint back in my locker and went looking for Harry. He wasn't working on his painting. As I walked past the gym, I peeked in. There were only three people in the there, and energetic was not the word I would have selected to describe their activity level. There were a couple of people swimming. Harry wasn't one of them. There were several people in the front visitor's lounge watching the big TV. None of them seemed terribly interested in the History Channel documentary that was on.

I finally found Harry on the practice putting greens. There were four other guys out there, each having trouble getting the ball in the cup. When Harry saw me approaching the greens, he retrieved his ball and came toward me.

"Come to rescue me from futility?" he asked.

"If you need rescuing," I said.

"You okay?"

"Mostly. Sort of numb, I guess."

"Want to get some coffee?"

"Sure."

"The thing that bothers me," I said as we sat in the mostly deserted cafeteria, "is the coincidence factor."

Harry nodded. "Two people who appear to be healthy, who were part of the same senior community," he said, "die within a week of each other. On the surface, it would appear to be a coincidence. But allowing that it was merely a coincidence seems incredible to you and leaves you with no place to go, nothing to work with."

"Exactly."

"Coincidence is anathema in the eyes of all good investigators," Harry said.

"But sometimes coincidences are real."

"Sometimes."

"Is this one of those times?" I asked.

"I don't know. On the surface it seems to be. There's no evidence that anything out of the ordinary happened here."

"But I think there is."

"Make your case."

"Walter shouldn't have had a heart attack, and Lucile ..."

"Shouldn't have had a tumor," Harry said, saying what I didn't want to say.

"Am I being foolish?"

"Foolish? No. Not foolish."

"But you think their deaths may be just what they appear to be, two unrelated, naturally occurring events."

73

"There doesn't appear to be any evidence that suggests anything else," Harry said. After a moment Harry added, "But that doesn't mean there isn't any. It just means you haven't found it yet."

I considered him.

"You should pursue this," he said, "until you find what you're looking for or until you're satisfied that there's nothing there."

"Thank you."

"If you're really grateful, you could get me a small bowl of chocolate ice cream."

I went to the soft serve machine and got two small bowls of chocolate ice cream. As we ate, Harry asked, "Are you still concerned about Martha?"

I took a moment to think. "No. If Walter had been the only victim, maybe. But she had no reason to kill Lucile. Besides, even though she's a bossy, spiteful old bitty, I'm not sure she's got it in her to kill anyone."

"I agree," Harry said. "So having eliminated her, you can move on."

"Do you think it's someone here at Happy Trails?"

"I certainly hope not," Harry said. "These people are our friends. Even the crotchety ones. Be easier if we had more information. A tox screen or an autopsy report might explain what caused the heart attack and the brain tumor."

"But we don't."

"Nope. You'll have to do it the old fashioned way— ask a lot of questions and connect all the dots."

The subdued mood at Happy Trails continued unabated until Lucile's funeral, which was held at the same place where Walter's funeral was held. Lucile's sister-in-law came from New Jersey. The same minister preached pretty much the same sermon for Lucile he'd preached for Walter the week before. I wondered how much he was getting paid for doing a rerun. About half way through, Harry leaned over and whispered that he was going to complain to the funeral director.

Lucile's sister-in-law showed up at the funeral home and left right after the service. She didn't talk to anyone. Why'd she even bother coming? Her niece, Patricia, seemed nice, though.

Alice had snacks for everyone in the dining room, and most of us spent some time remembering Lucile. Harry and I had been at a table for four with Evelyn and Tom Bethel. They only visited with us for a few minutes because Tom had been diagnosed with liver cancer and was undergoing treatment, which made him weak. After they left to go to their apartment, Ed and Jimmy came over and sat down.

"So Lucile had a brain tumor."

"Yes," I said.

"And nobody knew it?"

"Apparently not."

"Seems like as it started to grow it would have given her headaches or something."

"Sometimes that happens," I said. "Depends on where the tumor is and whether or not it is pressing against any nerves."

"And this wasn't, so it didn't give her any headaches until it was too late?"

"It was a very fast growing tumor," I said.

"What would cause one to grow that fast?"

"That's a good question, Jimmy."

Ed, the more thoughtful of the two had been sipping his coffee, listening. "Jimmy's good at asking questions," Ed said.

"How else am I gonna learn?"

"Questions are good, Jimmy," Harry said. "And Harriet is pretty good at coming up with answers. But the question you asked is a hard one, and she's going to need a little more time to come up with the answer."

Jimmy nodded. "You don't think it was multivitamins, do you?"

"Do you take vitamins, Jimmy?"

"Yes."

"I'm pretty sure vitamins didn't have anything to do with it. You keep taking your vitamins."

Harry went to get more coffee and pie, and I noticed on the TV that a storm was moving in our direction. You can never tell about West Texas weather in March.

Chapter 17

The storm blew in ahead of schedule a little after seven. Harry and I were in our apartment watching TV. Well, the TV was on, but Harry was reading, and I was doing a jigsaw puzzle on my Kindle—my guilty pleasure. The storm was quite an event. Lots of thunder, lightning, and wind, and golf-ball-sized hail. The front edge of the storm pounded our side of Abilene for a good ten minutes, which is a long time when you're talking about golf-ball-sized hail. At one point, the lightning and thunder seemed to be simultaneous, which I always understood to mean that the storm was directly overhead.

At seven twenty there was a bright flash of lightening and a simultaneous explosion of thunder and everything went dark.

"The lightning must have knocked out a transformer," Harry said, "as he pulled a small flashlight from the drawer in the table that sat between our chairs.

"I'll light some candles," I said.

But just as I got them lit, the Happy Trails generator kicked in and we were once again bathed in light. I blew out the candles and sat back down … for about three minutes. Then there was another bright flash of lightning, more deafening thunder, and the lights were gone again.

"Lightning must have hit the generator, too," Harry said.

"I'll light the candles again," I said.

I always liked the way a room felt when candles were all the light you had. "Kind of romantic, isn't it?" I said.

"Uh-huh."

"Give you any ideas?"

"It does," Harry said. "But I think we should have sex instead."

The next morning there was still no power. It was quite a challenge to get my make-up on with only candlelight in the bathroom. I don't wear a lot of makeup, but putting on mascara when you almost can't see your eyes isn't a challenge for the easily frustrated.

At seven thirty, we got a text. Cybil called an emergency meeting and wanted everyone in the cafeteria in ten minutes to explain. She had been on the phone with the mayor, she said, and needed to pass along the bad news. The storm had been a real humdinger. The hail damage across the southern side of Abilene had been extensive. But worse than the hail was the lightning. It had hit a major transformer sending powerful surges through the lines, knocking out several other transformers as well. It would take at least three days to restore the power. In addition, the Happy Trails backup generator had taken a direct hit and was completely fried. It would take several days to replace it. So, since

Happy Trails could not be operated properly or safely without electricity, she had arranged for us to stay a two nearby hotels, Sandalwood Suites and Overnight Inn, that were situated next door to each other less than a mile away, and were just across the parking lot from Buck's Family Diner. We would be housed in the hotels, and meals would be provided at Buck's.

"Why do we have to be split up between two hotels?" Jimmy asked.

"Because neither hotel has enough rooms available to accommodate seventy-five additional people," Cybil explained.

"Do we get to pick where we stay?"

Cybil smiled sweetly, trying hard to be patient. "Unfortunately, I had to go ahead and provide a guest list. Alphabetical order. Last names A-M will be at Overnight Inn, N-Z will be at Sandalwood Suites."

"What time can we check in?"

"The staff at each location is working hard to accommodate us. So even though normal check-in is at three, we can check in at eleven o'clock this morning. Pack your bags for at least three days, go to Bucks for breakfast, and check in to your hotel at eleven."

"Ed and me know Jo Jo Buck," Jimmy said. "He's likely to try and charge us."

Still smiling—she was being a real trooper—Cybil said, "Just tell them you're from Happy Trails, and they'll give you a bill to sign."

On the way out of the cafeteria, I saw Linda. She'd probably come in early to make sure all the medication distributions that she and her assistants monitor were properly collected. Most of us see to our own medications, but a few needed the nursing staff to make sure they took their daily medicines.

She'd been talking to Cybil. As she stepped away, I said, "Long night or early morning?"

"Early morning. How are you doing?"

"We're good. Listen, I know you're probably not going to want to tell me this, but was Lucile on HRT?"

Linda considered me a moment before speaking. "You're not going to respect patient confidentiality, are you?"

"She's dead, so, no."

"Fine. No, she was not."

"You know why I'm asking?"

"Yes," Linda said.

"What do you think?"

"I think had the answer been yes, you'd have to consider it. But since she wasn't, there must have been some other cause."

Philip, a round little man with a round little head, round little eyes, and round little glasses, who was standing next to me said, "DDT."

"DDT," I said. "What do you mean?"

"The government uses DDT to spray for mosquitos. That's what gave Lucile the tumor. DDT."

Philip had lost his wife Gina a couple of years ago, and I don't think he ever fully recovered.

"Philip," I said, "the city of Abilene does not use DDT to kill mosquitos. DDT hasn't been used in ages."

"That's what they want you to think. But they're using it."

"You'll have to excuse me," Linda said, and walked away. Lots of people walked away from Philip.

"How do you know, Philip?"

"Everybody knows that."

"I don't know it, Philip."

"Now you do," he said. Leaning close and speaking softly, he said, "You're welcome."

Harry, who had been standing patiently by said, "Philip, go pack."

"Already packed. Packed last night. Knew this was coming. Been telling people this was coming for a long time. Right? You've heard me."

"We have," Harry said. "We'll see you on the other side, post-apocalyptic."

As we walked away, Philip said, "Go ahead, make fun. You'll be singing a different tune when they inject the implants."

Chapter 18

We puttered around our room, taking our time packing. We have two windows in our living room that are on an outside wall, so with the blinds open we had some natural light. Harry had one small canvas bag. I had two full-sized suitcases. Harry smiled when he saw them sitting by the door.

Bags in the back of the Suburban, we left for Buck's Family Diner a few minutes before nine under an absolutely clear and beautiful sky. It always amazes me how clear it is after a big storm blows through.

Buck's has been an Abilene favorite for home-style cooking for many years. The portions are generous, and the food is good. Breakfast is especially good. Harry loves the bacon they serve—thick and smoky. The place is decorated to look like an old bunkhouse: rough wood walls, a big fireplace, ranch and farm tools along with deer heads and trophy-sized fish mounted on the walls, wagon wheel chandeliers. The wait staff wear jeans, boots, and checkered shirts. Not in the least bit authentic if you knew anything about farming or ranching, but it still provided a nice ambiance.

We ate breakfast with Ed and Jimmy and told horror stories about weather we'd endured or had heard about from other people over the years. It still wasn't time to check-in yet, so I suggested we go to the mall. Other than the bookstore, Harry is not fond of the mall. But since he couldn't come up with something else to do for an hour, he agreed. He bought two books, and we had more coffee in the little coffee shop in the bookstore until it was time to go check in.

Our room was a standard mid-price hotel room: a king-sized bed, desk and chair, TV sitting atop the four-drawer dresser, a small open closet to hang up a few clothes, and a bathroom with a tub-shower combination and one sink. Adequate. Since we weren't paying for it, and it was only for a couple of days, it was fine.

After we unpacked, we went down to the lobby to see what was going on. Didn't appear to be anything going on. "Makes you appreciate all the activities we've got going on at Happy Trails, doesn't it?"

"Yeah, it does," Harry said.

At eighty-two, Harry likes routine. I knew the next few days would be challenging for him. But I also knew he'd make an effort not to get too grumpy.

"Let's find something fun to do," I said.

"Like what? You want to go to the shooting range?"

"I was thinking more like the zoo."

"The zoo?"

"It's a nice day out. It only takes a couple of hours. And afterward we can go to lunch."

"Okay," he said. "The zoo it is."

On the way, I called David and explained what had happened and told him where we'd be for the next few days. He said they'd gotten a lot of rain but no hail. He also offered to let us stay with him and Nikki, but I told him we were already checked into a room, and we'd be fine.

The zoo was fun. I always love looking at the animals. Afterward, even though we could eat for free at Buck's, we decided to go to Chili's. As we ate, I asked Harry for advice on how to proceed with my investigation.

"That's what this is now," he said, "an investigation?"

"What would you call it?"

"An inquiry, maybe."

"Okay. How would you go about making an inquiry?"

He smiled and put a french fry in his mouth. "If I understand where you're headed with this, you're wondering whether they might have been taking something that might have caused, in Walter's case, his heart attack, and in Lucile's case, her brain tumor. Is that right?"

"Yes."

"Then I'd start by interviewing people who knew them, asking if they were aware of whether Walter or Lucile were taking medication Linda did not know about."

Chapter 19

As we walked into the hotel lobby, Sharon Williams, a retired school principal, rushed over to us. "Did you hear about Wilson?" she asked.

"What about Wilson?"

"He had a stroke."

"We hadn't heard. How serious?"

"He collapsed in their room. They took him to Hendrick."

"How's Natalie?"

"Trying to be brave."

I looked at Harry. "We should go see them," I said.

"I'll go bring the Suburban around to the front."

Hendrick was the other hospital in town, part of a massive healthcare system that was one reason Abilene was on several lists of top ten cities to retire to. Housing is affordable here, and there's excellent health care all over the place.

It took ten minutes to get to 18th and Pine. Harry parked in the visitor's section of the parking lot, and we went in together. I asked at the desk about Wilson Bancroft, and they said he wasn't in a room yet. I asked where his wife would be waiting, and they said probably in the critical care unit waiting room on the second floor. We took the escalator up to the second floor and turned right. Natalie was there. She'd been an air force veterinarian, a colonel when she retired—a strong, confident woman. She didn't appear to be either at the moment. Cybil and Linda were sitting on either side of her.

Natalie stood when she saw us approaching. I went to her, and we hugged.

"I'm so sorry," I said. "We came as soon as we heard."

"Thank you for coming. He's still with the doctors."

She sat down, and I pulled a chair around so I could sit facing her. Harry sat down on the other side of Linda.

"What happened?" I asked.

"We were in our room and were just going to go down to play a game of 42 that Lydia had arranged. Wilson stood up, hesitated, had something that looked like a shiver, and fell down. I went to him, and he was out. I think he hit his head on the side of the chair as he fell. So I called 911. By the time they got there, he was coming around, but he couldn't speak or move. Well, he could move his left arm a little bit, but that's all. One of the EMTs said he might have had a stroke."

"I'm so sorry."

She nodded. "It was just such a shock to see him go down like that. He's always been so strong and so active."

"If it was a stroke," I said, "it may have been a light one, and he may be just fine."

She nodded. She had enough medical training to know that what I was saying might be true. Or it might not be true.

"How about some coffee or tea?" I said.

"Some coffee would be good."

Harry stood. "How do you like it?"

"Black."

He looked at Cybil and Linda. They shook their heads and Harry went off to get coffee.

"Now that Harriet's here," Cybil said to Natalie, "Linda and I need to get back. Dozens of things we need to check on."

"I understand," Natalie said. "Thank you for coming."

"Call me as soon as you hear something?"

Harry returned with coffee for three, and we waited with Natalie until the doctor came out with a report. As we waited, I couldn't help but wonder if this was going to be another unexpected tragedy. Had Wilson taken something that caused his stroke? But now wasn't the time to question Natalie.

Dr. Andrews, a young man in his late thirties, came out about half an hour later. "He had a mild stroke," the doctor said. "Left hemisphere, so it initially impacted his right side muscles and his ability to speak. But he's already responding well with some speech and some slight movement in his right arm and leg. Those are good signs. We'll have him in a room in a little while, and you can go see him. I'll have someone come and get you."

"So the prognosis is good?" Natalie asked.

"It is. He'll be here a few days, but if he makes the kind of progress he's already displayed, things look good."

87

"Oh, thank God."

We waited with Natalie until a nurse came to take her to Wilson's room. "We'll come back later tonight during visiting hours," I said. "If you need anything, call me."

On the way back to the hotel, Harry said, "I know you wanted to ask."

"I did. But it wasn't the right time. Maybe tonight."

"Are you aware of a drug that could induce a heart attack, a brain tumor, and a stroke?"

"All I found was that menotega stuff. Under certain circumstance, in some people it might cause a heart attack."

"What about a brain tumor?"

"There was no mention of a brain tumor."

"Stroke?"

"No. But maybe Wilson just had a stroke."

"Sure," Harry said. "That's possible."

"Just like it's possible that Walter just had a heart attack and Lucile just had a fast growing brain tumor," I said. My tone was probably a little sharper than it needed to be.

Harry kept his eyes on the road.

"I'm sorry," I said. "That was uncalled for."

"I understand. You're pretty sure something's not right about all of this, but you can't put your finger on it, and it's frustrating."

"Yes."

"Just be patient and keep at it."

Chapter 20

We went back to the hotel room, and Harry said he was going to the hotel pool to swim. "Okay," I said, "I'll be back later. I'm going to look for Elizabeth, Mildred, and Judith."

"The three mistresses."

"I wouldn't let them hear you say that if I were you."

I saw Mildred and Betty in the lobby. "Have either of you seen Elizabeth?"

"Last I saw her," Betty said, "was at lunch at Buck's."

That would have been a couple of hours ago.

"She's been alone a lot since Walter died," Mildred said. "She's probably off by herself somewhere. Can't say I blame her. Most people don't know how to deal with a grieving person. They think distracting you so you won't think about the loss is what you need. But it's not. There's a period of time where you need to be left alone so you can think and remember and grieve, and heal."

Mildred was right. But I wasn't interested in distracting or cheering Elizabeth up. I needed information about Walter, and she might be the one who had it. "If you see her, would you tell her I'm looking for her?"

"Sure."

I went over to the Overnight Inn, thinking maybe she was with someone there. No one had seen her. Maybe she was in her room. I checked. No answer. Then I remembered that for the past few days I had seen her sitting by herself in the cafeteria at Happy Trails drinking coffee. Maybe she was still at Buck's. I walked over to Buck's, and Elizabeth was there, sitting in the corner by herself, a cup of coffee on the table in front of her as she stared off into space.

"Mind if I join you?" I asked as I reached her table for two.

My questioned jolted her back into reality.

"Oh, hi, Harriet. Not at all. Have a seat. I was just sitting here thinking about Walter."

"I know. Sorry to intrude."

"You're not intruding. So what's new?"

"You hear about Wilson?"

"No."

"He had a stroke."

Her eyes filled with tears. I explained that the doctor was hopeful, and I suggested that she join us later when we go back to visit.

"Yes. I'd like that."

"Listen, I need to ask you something about Walter. You feel up to answering a question?"

"Sure."

"Did Walter say anything to you about taking any new medication?"

Her eyes moved away from mine as she thought. Shaking her head, she said, "I don't remember him saying anything to me about a new medication. In fact, I don't think he took any medication at all—blood pressure, cholesterol, nothing. The man was as healthy as a horse … At least, he appeared to be."

I nodded.

"Why?"

"I don't know. I'm just trying to get a handle on what happened. There doesn't seem to be any good way to explain his heart attack."

"Have you asked Marion or Judith?"

I guess I looked surprised at her question.

"I knew Walter was seeing other women. I had no claim on him, and neither did they. Walter was enjoying himself. I was happy that some of the time he enjoyed himself with me. The problem was that one day I woke up and realized I loved him."

I didn't say anything.

"Literally," she said. "One morning when I woke up, I realized I was in love with Walter. I could only hope that if he got around to making a choice, it would be me. As it turns out, he never got the chance to make a choice."

I didn't expect to ever be in the situation Elizabeth had been in. But if I ever was, I doubted I would be willing to be simply one of several lovers. She must have been terribly lonely and desperate. How sad.

I found Marion in her room at the Overnight Inn, watching *Fox News*. Marion is a retired academic, a sociology professor for years before she moved into administration. She was a dean when she retired. "I'd offer you coffee," she said, "but you have to get it in the lobby and bring it up."

"That's fine. Thanks."

"Here, sit here," she said, gesturing to the desk chair. "There's only one chair in these rooms."

I sat down in the chair, and she sat on the edge of the bed.

"You follow politics?" she asked.

"Yes. Harry more than me. But I keep up."

"I watch it all the time. Hooked on it. But the stupid liberals drive me crazy. Especially that new congresswoman. The young one. You know who I mean.

"I know who you mean. She gets a lot of media coverage."

"Dumber than a bag of rocks. They say she graduated cum laude in economics from some fancy school in the east. If that's true, they ought to revoke that school's accreditation because she doesn't know anything about how an economy works. My blood pressure would probably go down if I'd quite watching the news about that kind of stuff."

I smiled.

"So, what's up?"

"I was wondering if you remember Walter mentioning anything to you about taking any new medication?"

She thought. "No, I don't think he did. Of course, most of the time we spent together we weren't talking. Especially about medications."

I wasn't sure how to respond to that, so I didn't.

"Why do you ask? You think he was taking something that caused his heart attack?"

"I don't know. That's why I'm asking."
"Probably good that someone's asking."

Chapter 21

Since Judith's last name was Pearson, she was in the same hotel Harry and I were in. I found her in the exercise room walking on the treadmill. She was a real exercise hound. Always doing something physical. It showed. She was trim and in good shape for a woman nearly eighty. Her skin still fit her body. She was wearing a snug-fitting workout suit that accentuated her assets, both top and bottom.

"Can you do that and talk at the same time?" I asked.

"Kind of like asking me if I can walk and chew gum at the same time."

Judith often tended toward sarcastic.

I smiled. "I meant, is it too difficult to maintain your pace and carry on a conversation. Some people would find it difficult. The breathing and all."

"I know what you meant. I was just yanking your chain. What do you need?"

I asked her the same question I'd asked Elizabeth and Marian. She gave me the same answer.

"Just out of curiosity, what did you and Walter talk about?"

"Politics, economics, philosophy."

"Really."

"Walter was a smart guy. Knew a lot about a lot of different things. You don't get to be as rich as Walter was without having something going on upstairs."

She had a point.

By the time I got back to our room, Harry had finished his swim, showered and dressed, and was sitting in the desk chair, reading. "Any luck?" he asked as I closed the door behind me.

I climbed onto the bed and propped the pillows up behind me so I could sit up. "Apparently Walter didn't talk about medications when he was with his girlfriends."

Harry smiled. "What did he talk about?"

"If he talked, he talked about serious stuff: philosophy, politics, economics."

"That's why I didn't play golf with him very often. Couldn't ever get him to shut up about that stuff so we could discuss important things."

"Such as?"

"Sex, football, fishing."

"I know you're kidding, but lots of men are like that. That's the only stuff they think about."

Harry got up and came over and kissed me on the cheek. "The stuff dreams are made of."

"Uh-huh. If he didn't play golf with you, who did he play with?"

"He and Stan were golfing buddies."

"Stan Albright?"

"Uh-huh. And he was also a regular at the Tuesday night poker game."

"There's a Tuesday night poker game?"

"I don't know. Is there?"

"You just said there was." I got up off the bed.

"No, I didn't. You didn't hear anything like that from me."

He put his arms around me and we stood facing each other. I liked it.

"What is it," I said, "some kind of illegal gambling thing?"

"Well, since I don't have any knowledge of whatever it is you're talking about, I can't really say. But I suspect that if such a thing existed, it would be just a friendly game that the guys involved would rather keep quiet."

"Why?"

"Because when men get together to play poker it's not like women getting together to play hand and foot. They're playing for money, and it's serious."

"How much money?"

"Probably a two-dollar betting limit."

"Two dollars."

"I don't know. I'm just guessing."

"Right. Why even bother?"

"Makes it more fun."

"Why aren't you part of this Tuesday night group?"

He kissed me. "Because I'd rather spend my Tuesday nights with you."

I liked that too.

"So who are these Tuesday night gamblers?"

"I don't know."

"Harry."

"It's a secret."

"Harry."

"Fine. Will Pendergrass, Ted Zemraski, and Kyle Johnson. Walter was the fourth."

"Do their wives know their husbands gamble every Tuesday night?"

"It's a closely guarded secret. So, probably."

Judy Pendergrass was in my ceramics class, and we had either lunch or dinner with them quite often, so I thought I'd start with Will. If we'd been at Happy Trails there'd be lots of places he might be, lots of things he might be doing. But options at the hotel were considerably more limited. I went to their room. No one answered my knock. I figured I'd give the pool a shot. Both Will and Judy were there. Will is a big man, probably six-four, two-fifty. Judy is five-four and weighs one-ten. I asked if I could join them.

They asked about Wilson. I told them what I knew. Then, "So, Will, I understand you and Walter were friends."

Will nodded. "Knew Walter for a lot of years."

"He ever mention any new medication he was taking?"

"You mean other than Viagra?"

Judy said, "Walter was taking Viagra?"

"The secret to his success."

"Did he need it," Judy asked, "or was he just trying to … *up* his game so to speak?"

"I don't know if he needed it or not," Will said, "but he certainly used it. His exploits were on the verge of becoming legend."

"Uh-huh," Judy said. "That why Charlie started using it? Or was he just trying to keep *up* with Walter?"

Will smiled.

As entertaining as their little routine was, it wasn't providing me with the information I needed. I said, "And you're sure he never mentioned any other medication he was taking?"

Will saw that I was serious. He thought. Shook his head. "Never did. You think his heart attack could have been the result of an interaction between stuff he was taking?"

"I've no idea. At this point I'm just asking questions."

Chapter 22

Maybe Kyle Johnson would know something. I asked the Happy Trails people I saw wandering around the hotel lobby if they had seen him. None had. But since his last name was Johnson, he would be next door at the Overnight Inn. At least that's where his room would be.

His wife Cindy answered my knock. "No, Kyle's not here. I expect him back soon, though. He said we'd go over to Buck's for dinner at five thirty."

"Okay. I just have a question to ask. I'll come by your table after dinner."

Harry and I walked over to Buck's at five twenty. Some of the tables in Buck's are small two or four-person tables. Others are long picnic tables pushed together end to end so that they will seat fifteen or twenty on each side of the table. Harry and I found a couple of spots at one end of a long table next to Neal and Patricia Simms. They'd been high school teachers. Neal had taught history; Patricia, after her kids were all in school, taught music. They had five children and fourteen grandkids. As we ate, she took out her phone and showed us the latest pictures and videos of their grandkids. Then Neal had a story to tell.

"So Julie," Neal says, smiling, "the nine-year-old, says, 'Grandpa, why are farts funny?'"

Harry chuckled.

"And I said, I don't know. Why do you think farts are funny? And Julie says, 'I don't think farts are funny. Eddie thinks farts are funny. He farts and then he laughs.' Eddie is the seven-year-old," Neal explained. "So I said, did you ask Eddie why he thinks farts are funny? And Julie says, 'Yes. He thinks farts are funny because girls don't want anyone to know they fart. So when they do, it's funny. But I told him that was wrong because Mom doesn't seem to mind.'"

We all laughed. Nothing like a good fart joke to put everyone in a good mood.

I looked around the room and saw Kyle and Cindy. Kyle was mostly bald and kept what little hair he still had cut very short. The sad thing was that Cindy was nearly as bald. But she wore a wig—a blond Marilyn Monroe wig. She wore eye makeup and lipstick that she thought went with the wig. It didn't, but it wasn't my place to tell her. The other couple sitting with them at a table for four were just leaving, so I told Harry I'd be back in a few minutes. I sat down with them, and Cindy said, "Harriet wants to ask you something."

"Yes," Kyle said, "I'll dance with you, but only if you let me lead."

"You can't lead," I said. "You have two left feet."

"That's what I keep telling him," Cindy said.

Once we got the silliness out of the way, Kyle said, "So what is it you want to know?"

100

"Did Walter ever mention to you that he was taking new medication of any kind?"

"Not that I remember. But why would he?"

"Because you were poker buddies."

Kyle was very still for a moment. Then he said, "What?"

"I'm sorry," I said. "That was supposed to be a secret, wasn't it?"

"I ... uh ... I'm sorry. Secret? I don't ..."

"Oh, for Pete's sake, Kyle. Everybody knows about your stupid poker game. Get over it."

"What?"

Cindy said, "Forget the poker game, you old sneak. Did Walter tell you anything about any medications he was taking?"

Annoyed that he'd been found out, "No, he didn't. And who told you about our game? Probably Harry. The old blabbermouth."

I smiled. "In all fairness to Harry, I had to twist his arm to get it out of him."

"You can't trust anybody to keep a secret."

Marilyn was still working on her dessert when I made it over to where she was sitting. "I was hoping to be able to ask Ted a question about Walter," I said.

"Sure. He'll be back in a while. Went to the men's room. Takes him forever to empty his bladder. One of those old man things, I guess. You might as well have another cup of coffee."

When Ted returned, he looked tired.

"Harriet wants to ask you a question about Walter," Marilyn said.

"What about the water?"

""Not water," Marilyn said, impatiently and with increased volume. "Walter. Walter."

"Oh. Sure. What about him?"

"I was wondering if Walter said anything to you about his medication?"

Ted shook his head. "I don't think Walter was into meditation."

"Not meditation," Marilyn said loudly, "medication. What kind of medication was he taking? Pills."

"Oh. Nope. Walter never said anything to me about any medication he was taking. Don't know if he took anything at all. Walter was pretty healthy. I take a whole handful every morning. But I don't know if Walter did or not."

"I don't either," I said. "That's what I'm trying to find out. I thought he might have mentioned it during one of your poker games."

"What poker game?"

"One of your Tuesday night poker games," Marilyn said.

"We don't play poker."

"Ted, everybody knows you guys play poker on Tuesday nights," Marilyn said.

"No, they don't," he grumbled. Then, getting up from his chair, "Excuse me. I gotta go to the men's room again."

"You just went," Marilyn complained.

"And I gotta go again," he said, standing up. "Doggone prostate," he mumbled as he left.

I found Elizabeth sitting with Sharon. "You still want to go with us to see Wilson and Natalie?"

She did. I said she should meet us in the lobby in thirty minutes.

Elizabeth was ready, and it took us ten minutes to get across town to Hendrick.

"He's getting better," Natalie said excitedly as the three of us entered. She was like a kid who got what she wanted for Christmas.

"How you feeling, Wilson?" Harry asked.

He nodded, and after only a slight hesitation said, "Better. I can talk, and the muscles on my right side are starting to work again. The doctor says a few weeks of physical therapy and I'll be able to go fishing again."

"Good," Harry said. "Glad to hear it."

"The doctor said it was a mild stroke," Natalie explained. "He did a special kind of MRI on him earlier this afternoon and said there didn't appear to be any damage. So he should be okay."

Elizabeth had tears in her eyes. "That's really good, Nat. You're a lucky woman."

Wanting to lighten things up a bit, Harry asked Wilson, "So do you have a good looking nurse?"

"Some big, hairy, bald guy," Wilson said.

"Jeez," Harry said. "What's the world coming to?"

Chapter 23

The next morning, the only person left on my list was Stan Albright, Walter's golfing buddy. The whole process of finding and talking to people would have been easier if we had been at Happy Trails where we belonged. But we weren't. So I looked for Stan at Buck's where I hoped he was eating breakfast. He wasn't. Maybe he'd been there earlier.

Harry and I ate and went back to our room. "Think I'll go for my swim," Harry said. "Want to come along?"

"You think Stan might be there?"

"He might. He prefers swimming to the exercise room."

"Okay. But I don't think I'll swim. I don't want to have to do my hair again. I'll bring a book."

It was a nice spring day, already in the low seventies at ten after nine. Harry dove in and started his laps. The pool at Happy Trails was quite a bit bigger, but as far as Harry was concerned, even a small pool was better than no pool at all. He would just swim more laps.

Several people were sitting around the pool, enjoying the morning sun. One of them was Emily Hopkins, wearing a skimpy two-piece swimsuit, watching Harry as he swam. Emily was nice enough. What bothered me about her was that at seventy-five she could still pull off wearing a skimpy two-piece bikini—tight, toned skin, big chest, a small behind, and an actual waistline. Probably had some kind of mutant DNA. She looked at me and smiled. Nodding toward Harry she said, "Not bad for an old geezer of eighty-two."

"Just remember, he's my old geezer."

"Don't have to worry about me, Harriet. Good looking men like Harry are nice to look at. But I've had four husbands, and I'm not the least bit interested in having another man to deal with."

I looked around the pool area. No Stan, but I sat down to read anyway. I had been reading and Harry swimming about thirty minutes when Stan came out to the pool area in his swimming trunks. Unlike Harry, who has a flat belly, Stan had a bit of a stomach. Emily paid him no mind. I went over to him and said, "You're just the guy I was looking for. Got a minute?"

"Let me guess, you're getting tired of that old reprobate and are looking for a young stud."

"You're two years older than Harry."

"Age is simply a state of mind."

"It doesn't appear that your body is aware of that."

"Ouch. That was unkind. If you're going to insult me, we should sit down.

We sat at a table that had an umbrella over it.

"Want something to drink?" Stan asked.

"No, thank you. I understand that you were Walter's golfing buddy."

"Walter was the only golfer at Happy Trails that was as bad as I was. I'm gonna miss him."

"Maybe some of the ladies will let you play with them."

"I don't know. My good looks might throw them off their game."

"It would be a struggle for them, I'm sure."

"So what did you want to know about Walter?"

"Did he ever say anything to you about medication he was taking?"

Stan thought and shook his head. "Not that I can remember. Not really the kind of stuff men talk about while they play golf. Or anything else for that matter. Why? You trying to make sense out of his heart attack?"

"Yeah."

"Me, too. And I'm coming up empty. Walter was a healthy guy. Ate right, exercised. Last guy I would have expected to have a heart attack."

"Me, too. And you're sure he never said anything about any meds he was taking."

"I'm sure. There was one conversation where he mentioned something he'd read about a new miracle drug. Something supposed to rejuvenate your cells. Make you young again. Add decades to your life."

"Really."

"Yeah. We were on the golf course, and I was complaining about getting old. He mentioned this article he'd read. But he didn't saying anything about taking anything. He said he'd seen it in a magazine or something.

Maybe in the AARP magazine, or one of those health magazines. It was just small talk while we were playing golf."

"Did he mention the name of this drug?"

"If he did, I don't remember it."

"Was it menotega?"

Stan repeated the name. "I don't think I've ever heard of that. And like I said, I don't think he mentioned the name. You think he was taking something that caused his heart attack?"

"I don't know. Maybe."

"What about Lucile's tumor?"

"Yeah, I'm wondering about that, too."

Chapter 24

For normal paying customers, the hotel served a free breakfast in a nice room off the lobby with comfortable tables and chairs. In the mornings, it was a beehive of activity. In the evening, however, it was just an empty room. Several of us decided it was just right for playing cards, so we appropriated it, pushed a couple of the small tables together, and had ourselves a game room.

Mac and Estelle Bradford, who live in the apartment next door to us at Happy Trails, came over from the Overnight Inn to play Shanghai with us. It's a complicated game where each of the ten hands requires you to collect a different combination of cards. It takes a good deal of concentration and focus. But Estelle would rather tell stories than focus on the game, which means it takes longer to play, and we have to constantly remind her what she needs for a given hand. But she's a sweet lady, and Mac and Harry are buddies, so we try to be patient with Estelle.

We finished the tenth hand a little after nine. Harry, as usual, had the lowest score. Estelle somehow managed to come in second. I had the highest score. I hate when that happens. By nine thirty we were in our room watching the *Ingram Angle* ... sort of. Harry had his phone out checking Facebook; I was working a jigsaw puzzle on my Kindle. At ten minutes to ten, someone knocked on the door. Harry answered it. It was Elizabeth. She said, "Georgette was just taken to the hospital."

I stepped up behind Harry. "What happened?"

"She lost sight in her left eye."

"Where did they take her?"

"Regional Medical."

I looked at Harry. "We need to go."

Harry nodded.

"Can I go with you?" Elizabeth asked.

"Of course."

Harry went to pull the Suburban around to the front entrance. I grabbed my sweater and purse, while Elizabeth went to do the same.

Georgette Wibly is seventy-nine and is as nice as can be. And she's healthy. She looks little-old-lady frail, but on the tennis court is surprisingly strong and agile. Why would she suddenly lose sight in her left eye? Something must have happened on the right side of her brain, impacting the optic nerve to her left eye.

It took all of five minutes to get to the hospital. After forty years of being a cop in Abilene, Harry knew every street and alley in the city, and knew how to get anywhere quickly. I'd worked at Regional as a surgical nurse for thirty years and knew most everyone who was still on staff. The ER nurse was Charlene Whisky, a petite, soft spoken woman.

"Georgette?" I said to her.

"Dr. Lipsky is examining her now. I'll let you know as soon as I know something."

Elizabeth, Harry, and I stepped into the ER waiting room. Oscar, Georgette's husband, was already there. "How you doing, Oscar?" Harry asked.

"I don't know. Wasn't expecting anything like this."

"How about some coffee?"

"Sure. Coffee'd be good."

Harry went to get four coffees, and I sat down next to Oscar. "What happened?" I asked.

"We were watching TV and she didn't look good. Said the right side of her head hurt." Oscar put his hand up to his head to show me where her pain had been. "Then she said her left eye was hurting and the pain was getting worse. Then, all of the sudden, she said she couldn't see out of her left eye. That's when I called 911."

"I'm sorry," I said.

"You're a nurse. What does that sound like to you?"

"I don't know. Obviously something going on in her brain, but …"

"Like with Lucile," Oscar said. He was frightened.

"Doesn't mean the same thing is happening to Georgette. She's with the doctor now. We need to wait and see what he's able to find."

Harry returned with coffee for four. Forty-five minutes later Charlene came in and said the doctor would be out to see us in a few minutes.

Dr. Lipski looked to be in his early thirties. I knew he was older than that and that he was very good at his job.

"All I can tell you right now," he said, "is that the optic nerve of her left eye is not functioning normally. I don't know why. She does not have any of the normal issues associated with loss of vision in one or both eyes. We'll do an MRI first thing in the morning. I want to keep her overnight."

"I'm staying with her," Oscar said.

"I've given her something to calm her down and help her sleep," the doctor said. "Best thing for you to do is go home and get some sleep yourself."

"Nope. I'm staying with her in her room."

The doctor started to object, but realized Oscar needed to stay.

"I'll make sure someone comes to get you," he said, "when we have her settled in a room."

I followed the doctor into the hallway. Once the door had closed behind us, I said, "Have you heard about Lucile?"

"I did."

"Brain tumor," I said.

"All we can do is wait until there's an MRI to look at. Go home and get some sleep."

Chapter 25

Harry was asleep almost immediately. He always went to sleep within seconds of his head hitting the pillow. It had been that way for over fifty-five years. I lay in the dark and thought about what was going on. Two apparently healthy people had died suddenly. Wilson had a stroke, and now Georgette had something going on in her brain. The more I thought about Wilson, the more I thought he simply had a stroke and he would be okay. This thing with Georgette, though, scared me. I could imagine how Oscar felt. If something like this happened to Harry, I'd be a basket case. I was trying to stay positive, but given what happened to Lucile … I found myself hoping Georgette made it through the night.

At some point I must have drifted off, because the next thing I knew, I was looking at the bedside clock, and it said seven twelve am. Harry was in the shower. I checked my iPhone. No messages about Georgette. No news was good news. Harry was done in the bathroom at seven twenty, and I was in and out in twenty-two minutes, including hair and makeup. Not bad.

We went to Buck's for breakfast, getting there a little before eight, and left for the hospital as soon as we were done at eight twenty. I asked at the front desk about Georgette. They said she was scheduled for an MRI at eight forty-five, and we could wait over there.

We made our way through the maze of hallways to the MRI area with all their signs warning of a magnetic zone. Oscar was already there.

"They told me I should come over here and wait," Oscar said. "They're bringing her down now."

"You get any sleep last night?"

"I dozed off for a few minutes at a time all night long. I think they buy those crappy chairs on purpose to discourage family from wanting to spend the night."

"Down right inconsiderate," Harry said. "You eaten yet? Had coffee?"

"They brought me a tray when they brought Georgette's."

"That was nice of them," I said, trying to offset Harry's remark. I had, after all, spent my whole adult working life as part of this hospital staff. I tended to be more forgiving of their imperfections than Harry was.

"You need more coffee?" Harry asked Oscar.

"Another cup of coffee would be good," he said.

"You want more coffee?" he asked me.

I didn't, and he left.

"Why is this stuff happening?" Oscar asked me.

"I don't know."

With tears in his eyes, Oscar said, "What if she dies like Lucile did?"

Just about broke my heart. "Oscar, we have to have faith. The doctors will do everything they can to find out what's wrong and fix the problem."

"And if the worst happens?"

"If the worst happens, when it comes, we'll face it. But Georgette is not dead, and there's no point worrying about what will happen when she does pass on. No point at all. So pray about it and get yourself into a positive frame of mind. She's going to need you to be at your best to help her deal with whatever's wrong."

He nodded and took a deep breath. "You're right. I need to be positive and focus on helping her get through this."

Harry came back with two coffees. As we waited, he talked to Oscar about his favorite subject—politics—hoping to keep his mind off the obvious. But I knew that even though Oscar appeared to be engaged in the subject, he was still, in another part of his mind, worried about his wife.

At nine thirty-eight the MRI technician, a nice young man with both his arms covered in tattoos, came out and told us that the MRI went well and that Georgette was being taken back to her room.

"Dr. Greenberg," the tech said, "he's the neurologist, will have it in a few minutes. He'll study it and then consult with Dr. Bascom. Then they'll come by your wife's room later and talk to you and her about it."

Oscar thanked him and said, "Well, I need to get back to the room. Thank you for coming."

"Call us after the doctor's come in to talk to you, or if you need anything at all."

As we drove back to the hotel, I decided that I needed to talk with Lucile's friends just as I had with Walter's. See if she was taking anything new. I had thought about asking Oscar if Georgette was, but figured it was not the time. Lucile had depended on me for some things, but other than that we weren't that close. There were other ladies that she spent time with: Gwinn Baker and Gillie Brooks were probably her closest friends. I found myself hoping that Lucile had been taking something and that she mentioned to them what it was.

Chapter 26

Gwinn Baker's husband died two years ago, and there was a substantial insurance policy. She didn't really need it because Harley Baker's fifteen fast food restaurants continued to bring in plenty of money. As far as Gwinn was concerned, the insurance money was discretionary income she could do with as she saw fit. And what she enjoyed was shopping for jewelry. However, even though she has lots of money, she's no fool about how she spends it. When I asked if anyone knew where she was, I was told she was shopping. What that meant was that she was in her Mercedes hitting all the pawn shops in town, and there are a lot of them in Abilene, looking for deals on glittery baubles. She had discovered that when people find themselves in need of cash, they often pawn guns, tools, and jewelry. And if you were good at haggling, you could get good stuff at ten cents on the dollar. At least that's what she claimed. Harry said it was more like fifty cents on the dollar. Still, it was a good discount though.

I knew if Gwinn were out shopping, she'd wouldn't be back until after lunch. So I went looking for Gillie Brooks. I found her in the exercise room at the Overnight Inn where she was staying. Exercise—got to keep the legs moving and the heart pumping. That's the theory anyway.

"Hi, Harriet," Gillie said as I came up alongside the treadmill. "I wondered when you get around to me."

"Yeah? How come?"

"Because you've been asking Walter's friends if he mentioned anything to them about medications he was taking. Since Lucile's death was as unexpected as Walter's, and happened in such close proximity to his, I figured you'd be asking Lucile's friends about her medications."

"Good thinking. So what's the answer?"

"I don't remember her discussing her medications at all. If she was taking something new, she didn't tell me about it."

"Okay, thanks."

"You really think some sort of chemical interaction caused her brain tumor?"

"It's possible."

"No kidding. Every commercial on TV about medication always includes a big list of possible interactions. Some of them even include death. Why would someone take medication that could kill them? And why would doctors prescribe crap like that anyway?"

"I think the chances of a serious and dangerous interaction are usually very low."

"But there is still a chance," Gillie said.

"Yes."

"Wouldn't catch me taking any of that kind of stuff."

"Yeah, it's kind of a mystery, isn't it?"

"You ask Linda about Lucile?"

"I did."

"And?"

"She couldn't say. Confidentiality."

"Uh-huh. Lucile's dead. She doesn't care about confidentiality anymore. Linda probably told you and then made you promise not to tell."

"You and Lucile were close," I said. "If she was taking something but didn't tell you, why would she have told Linda?"

Gillie considered me for a moment as she kept up her mile-in-thirty-minutes pace. "Maybe," she said. "All I know is one of my best friends is dead and ..."

Her voice caught. She took a deep breath.

"... and I miss her, and I'm pissed about it. So if you can, you find out why this happened and don't let it happen to anyone else."

Chapter 27

Okay, so my current strategy wasn't getting me anywhere. If Walter or Lucile were taking anything that wasn't part of their standard medication regimen, they weren't telling anyone. But what about Georgette? I hadn't wanted to ask Oscar because he was so upset. But maybe I should go ahead and ask him.

It was getting close to lunchtime, so I crossed the big shared parking lot back to the Sandalwood Suites. It was a near perfect spring day—temperature in the mid seventies, clear sky, no wind. Would be a nice day to be on the lake, and I knew Harry would be thinking about it. I doubted, though, that he'd bring it up. He knew I'd go with him if he asked me to, but he also knew that all this was weighing heavily on my mind and that I needed to stay focused on it. So he'd forego the lake so I could keep working on this, even though I wasn't making any headway. Harry's a dear man. I love him so.

Harry was in our room. He'd had his thirty-minute swim, had showered and dressed. I gave him a kiss on the lips.

"What was that for?"

"Just because I love you."

"Yeah? How much?"

"You'll have to settle for the kiss right now. It's lunchtime and then we need to go to the hospital."

"Not a big fan of quickies, are you?"

"You can wait until tonight. Now take me to Buck's and feed me."

I had a salad; Harry had a turkey and bacon club. It was a huge sandwich. I'd have been lucky to get half of it down. I told him about my conversation with Gillie, and that I still needed to get with Gwinn. "You're in luck, then," Harry said, "because she just walked in."

When I finished my salad, Harry said, "Go talk to Gwinn. I'll sit here and have more coffee."

The waiter had just left Gwinn when I sat down opposite her. "Find any new baubles this morning?"

She held up her right hand and wiggled her third finger. A beautifully cut emerald shimmered in a sparkling gold setting.

"Nice," I said. "Did Lucile ever talk to you about any medication she was taking?"

She took a moment to think. "No," she said finally. "Not that I remember. I would have been surprised if she had. Lucile didn't talk about stuff that most people would categorize as private."

Before the conversation went any further, Lizzy Alef sat down with us. "I can't believe Cybil couldn't find us a better place to eat," she said.

"Why?" I asked. "What's wrong?"

"What's wrong? Have you not had a cup of coffee?"

"Yes."

"Then you know what's wrong. It's strong enough to walk out under it's own power." Lizzy is the official Happy Trails grump.

"I thought it was pretty good coffee," I said.

"Good?"

"It's a subjective consideration, isn't it?"

"Subjective consideration," she said, derisively. "That's a laugh. The lettuce in my salad was wilted. I suppose that's a subjective consideration as well."

"Is there anything about Buck's you like?" I asked.

"Sure. My waiter was a nice young man with a cute butt. What's that on your finger?" she asked Gwinn.

Gwinn held up her hand and said, "My latest acquisition."

Lizzy studied it from across the table. "Probably could have fed a family of thirty-seven Africans with what you paid for that."

Lizzy is not only a grump, she's also judgmental and hypocritical—a delightful combination of traits that endears her to everyone she meets.

"I send three hundred dollars a month," Gwinn said, "to Food for a Hungry World. How much do you contribute?"

Lizzy smiled. "Good for you. You married well, and you can afford it. It's the least you can do." She stood. "Well,

121

it's been nice chatting with you both, but I've got the find the manager and complain about the service here."

As she walked away, Gwinn said, "She has no idea what she's like, does she?"

"I don't think so."

"And if anyone tried to tell her, she wouldn't believe it."

Harry and I went to Hendrick first to see Wilson. He was better. I could see the relief in Natalie. "The doctor said if he keeps making this kind of progress, he can go home in a day or two."

Harry and I chatted with them for a few minutes, and I told them they were in our prayers.

On the way across town to Regional Medical, Harry said, "So what do you think about Wilson's stroke?"

"You mean in relation to Walter, Lucile, and Georgette? "

"Yeah."

"I think Wilson just had a stroke. It happens a lot to people in their eighties."

"Well, that's a cheerful thought," he said.

"Yeah, the truth can be a wonderful thing."

Oscar was in the room with Georgette, sipping a cup of coffee. I leaned across the bed and gave Georgette a kiss on the cheek. "You doing okay?"

"I'm scared," she said. "Other than when I had Judy, I've never been in a hospital."

I took her hand. "They'll take good care of you here," I said. "Dr. Greenberg is very good at his job. One of the best."

"He was here a little while ago," Oscar said. "Bascom was with him. The MRI showed a tumor pressing on the optic nerve. That's why she can't see out of her left eye. He wants to do surgery right away."

"Brain surgery," she said, obviously frightened.

"It sounds scary," I said. "But it's not as big a deal as it used to be." That, of course, was a lie. Brain surgery is always a big deal. But that's not what either of them needed to hear. "If I needed brain surgery," I said, "I'd want Greenberg doing it."

"He said the chances were good," Oscar said. "Didn't sound that encouraging to me."

"There's always a risk involved," I said. "But doing nothing is not an option." I was still holding Georgette's hand. I gave it a squeeze.

"That's what the doctor said."

"In your place," I said, "I'd agree to the surgery." Before my words died away, Georgette squeezed my hand, jerked, went rigid for a moment, and then began convulsing. I stepped out into the hallway and shouted, "Code blue."

The nurses immediately began scrambling and I told Harry and Oscar that we needed to get out of the way. We went out into the hallway just as three nurses rushed in with a crash cart.

"What's happening?" Oscar said, horrified at what he was witnessing.

"They'll do everything they can to save her."

123

Chapter 28

Harry and Oscar and I were in the waiting room nearest Georgette's room. I'd told her nurse where we would be.

Oscar was a wreck. Perfectly understandable. If something unexpected like that happened to Harry, I'd be basket case. I wanted to ask him my question about Georgette taking any new medication, but given the shape he was in I didn't want to ask him right then.

Harry usually fetches the coffee while I stay with whoever needs some company. But this time I felt Harry needed to sit with Oscar. A guy thing. So I went for three coffees. As I made my way to the cafeteria where I could get three decent cups of coffee, I found myself struggling to hold back the tears. Two friends had died about a week apart and another one was in jeopardy. I knew—couldn't prove, but knew—that natural causes was not the explanation for what had happened. The problem was I didn't know what the actual cause was. I'm a nurse not a detective, I told myself. I don't have the skills to pull this off. But no one else seemed to think there was anything amiss. Harry was trying to be supportive, and I appreciated his efforts, but even he wasn't convinced there was anything beyond natural causes involved. If anything was to be done, it was up to me.

I got three coffees, put lids on them, put them in a carrier, paid for them, and headed back toward the waiting room. There had to be something causing all this. Or someone. Probably some one using some thing. Maybe. Why would anyone want to do this sort of thing? What possible motive could there be? The only connection between Walter, Lucile, and Georgette is Happy Trails. Do the deaths and illnesses have something to do with Happy Trails? I couldn't imagine what it might be. To me, the most likely scenario was that the three of them were taking a medication that generated some serious negative side effects. That's what I thought. Okay, but why did I think that? Because when you get a bunch of old people together who are taking all sorts of medications there are bound to be some negative side effects. But doctors who prescribe medications watch the interaction-side effect thing pretty closely. So if they were taking something that caused a deadly side effect, maybe it was not something a doctor prescribed. What would it have been, and where would they have gotten it?

As I started down the long corridor to the waiting room I thought of Linda. She managed all the prescription meds for Happy Trails residents. Even if you didn't need help keeping track of and taking your medications, all of them were purchased though a mail-order company. Doing it that way saved us money, but they were sent to each resident in care of Happy Trails. Linda would then open and inspect each package to make sure it was the correct medicine in the correct dosage. So theoretically, everything that residents at Happy Trails took came through her office. And she worked closely with Dr. Bascom. Could the two of them be in cahoots in some sort of scheme? Theoretically, I suppose. But again, what would the motive be? Money. That sort of thing is always about money. But would two people I knew and counted among my friends give others of my friends something that could produce deadly side effects in them? It just didn't seem likely.

Well, crap. Maybe I was imagining all this. Maybe Walter just had a heart attack. And maybe Lucile just developed a fast growing brain tumor that killed her. And maybe, at the same time, Georgette also developed a brain tumor that was endangering her life. Maybe it was all just coincidental. Sure. And maybe I'm the Easter Bunny.

As I stepped into the waiting room I knew I needed to talk to Linda again. But for now Oscar and Georgette were the more immediate concern.

Chapter 29

It was one thirty, about thirty minutes after Georgette's seizure. No one had had much to say. The hospital Chaplin came in and asked if he could have a prayer with us. Oscar said yes. The Chaplin asked who he would be praying for and what the situation was. He listened patiently as Oscar explained. He led a nice prayer, shook Oscar's hand, and told him to call on him if there was anything he could do.

At five after two, a few minutes after the Chaplin left, the nurse came out. "Dr. Greenberg has decided to do emergency surgery to remove the tumor. The surgery will take four to six hours."

Oscar nodded. Other than that, he appeared to be numb with shock. I called several Happy Trails people and told them what was going on. They said they would spread the word.

At ten of five, Harry said, "Its dinnertime. You hungry?"

"Not really," Oscar said.

"You need to keep up your strength. You ought to eat something."

"Okay."

"You want to eat in the cafeteria," Harry said, "or go somewhere and get something better than hospital food?"

"I don't want to leave Georgette," he said. "I'll eat in the cafeteria. If you two want to go someplace else, I understand."

"We'll stay with you," Harry said.

As we ate, I tried to get Oscar to talk about other things. He made an effort, probably just to be polite, but his heart wasn't in it.

When we got back to the waiting room, Oscar would sit for a while and then get up and pace. Then he'd sit, then he'd pace some more. I felt so bad for him. As we waited, I got to thinking about him and Georgette. She was the one who always had something good and encouraging to say. Not that Oscar was negative. He wasn't. But Georgette was always the one who seemed to be in the lead. Oscar had depended on her. He was a strong, capable man, but she had been his rock, his source of calm and assurance. Without her there to reassure him, he was worried and fretful. In his place, I would be too.

At eight fifteen, the doctor came out, looking tired. "We got all of the tumor," he said. "Her vitals are normal. I think she's going to be all right."

Oscar breathed deeply and tears began to stream down his face. He grabbed the doctor's hand and shook it. "Thank you so much."

"The optic nerve is grumpy," Dr. Greenberg said. "It doesn't like to be touched. It'll take a while before her vision returns to normal. But I believe it will."

"Thank you," Oscar said again.

"Had someone prescribed something new for her?" Greenberg asked.

"Not that I know of," Oscar said.

"Why?" I asked.

"Her blood work indicated that her system was somewhat out of balance. Increased levels in some areas, reduced levels in others. Nothing I can really put my finger on, but it just doesn't look right. We'll keep a close watch on it while she's here."

Oscar was nodding; I was thinking. *I knew it! Someone was giving her something.*

"She'll sleep for a couple more hours," Dr. Greenberg said. "You go home and get some sleep. Come back tomorrow."

Chapter 30

The next morning, Cybil called several residents, me being one of them, and explained that the electricity was back on and Happy Trails was in business again. We should call several other people and make sure that everyone knew we could go back home. Everyone was delighted.

By the time everyone got home and unpacked, it was nearly lunchtime. The food at Buck's Family Diner is good, but it isn't the same quality that Alice prepares for us, so we were all looking forward to lunch. She didn't disappoint. She served a delicious pot roast (she must have gotten up early and put it in the oven) with red potatoes, baby carrots, and onions. She baked yeast rolls to go with it. The dining room smelled heavenly, and to me it was a joyous homecoming celebration.

Just as Harry and I were transferring our plates from our trays to our table, Harry saw BettyJo Kendrick heading in our direction with her tray. I heard him give a low groan. BettyJo's husband, Ken, had passed away about year ago after a long bout with cancer. She was just getting back to normal, though all of us were having trouble pinning down what was normal for BettyJo. About six months after Ken passed away, BettyJo began having strange dreams that she believed were precognitive in nature. And of course, it was necessary for her to tell you all about what she had seen in her … dream-vision.

"Mind if I sit with you two?" BettyJo asked.

I smiled. "Not at all. Please join us."

"Hello, Harry,"

"Hi, BettyJo."

She put her plates on the table, and Harry offered to take her empty tray away for her.

"Have you heard anything about Georgette?"

"She's awake and responsive," I said as Harry came back to the table. "Oscar is with her. They'll keep her four or five days."

"She's lucky to be alive," BettyJo said. "But even if she survives this, she's only got a short time left."

"Why do you say that?"

"Because of what I dreamed."

"What did you dream?" Harry asked. I could hear the annoyance in his voice. I don't think BettyJo noticed.

"I dreamed about a traveling man in a long dark coat and a big western hat and cowboy boots who was passing out death certificates to people here in Abilene. He had a kiosk set up at the mall where he was serving Starbucks coffee and Krispy Cream donuts. A sign on the kiosk said *The Twilight Zone*, and every fifth person in line got a death certificate. Several of us from Happy Trails were in line for the free coffee and donuts, and Walter and Lucile and Georgette were in line and spread out so that each of them got a death certificate. I was two places in line behind Georgette, so I didn't get one. But as the man handed me my coffee and donut, he said, 'Nice to see you, BettyJo. Ken was here last year and collected his certificate. He wants you to know that he is enjoying himself immensely and is anxious to see you.'"

She smiled and dug into her pot roast. "Boy, this is really good," she said. "I like the food at Buck's, but no one can match Alice's cooking."

"How do you know he was a traveling man?" Harry asked. Out of all that BettyJo had said, I wasn't sure why he focused on that particular detail. Maybe it was one of his advanced investigative techniques. You know, ask about unimportant details and see what comes of it.

"I don't know," BettyJo said, "I just did. In the dream I knew that he traveled around handing out death certificates. And Walter and Lucile and Georgette each got one."

She took another bite and smiled.

"And since Walter and Lucile died," I said, "you think Georgette will also die."

"Yes. It's sad, isn't it?"

"I'll say," Harry said. He took a sip of coffee and asked, "When did you have this dream?"

"The night before Walter died."

I considered her for a moment. "Why didn't you say something sooner?"

"Because no one takes me seriously."

Oops. I didn't know if she'd picked up on that or not.

"So why mention it now?" I asked.

"Didn't want you to get your hopes up about Georgette."

Harry took a deep breath but didn't say anything. I said, "You really believe your dreams are a precognitive experience, don't you?"

"Some of the dreams I've had have come true."

"Some of them," Harry said.

BettyJo smiled.

"Have you had any dreams since then?" I asked.

"Oh sure. I dream every night. Last night I dreamed that I was the big boobed weather girl on channel six, and that James Bond called and told me that if I agreed to be the liaison between MI6 and the CIA, he'd take me out to dinner and show me a good time."

Harry just looked at her.

"Did you agree?" I asked.

"You bet I did."

"Which James Bond was it?" I asked.

BettyJo smiled. "Sean Connery."

Chapter 31

Everyone was happy to be home, but being home reminded everyone that two of our friends had died, and their rooms needed to be cleaned out, and new tenants had to move in. Fortunately, Cybil was sensitive to the emotional ups and downs of running a retirement village, and always scheduled to have the recently vacated apartments emptied and at least partially cleaned at night while friends and neighbors were asleep. The people she hired were professionals and understood why they were working at night. They also understood that some seniors are very light sleepers. They worked quickly but quietly, and usually the next morning no one had heard a thing. However, everyone knew the rooms had to be prepared for new occupants, sometimes painted and the carpets cleaned. What this amounted to was that not only were you aware that your friend had died, but that all traces of his or her presence were being eliminated. It was that reality that gave rise to the Resident's Wall. Just to the left of the main desk in the front entryway was a large wall where the photos of all Happy

Trails residents hung. When you came to Happy Trails, a formal photo was taken and hung on that wall with your name under it. That way, even when you were gone, when your apartment had been cleared out and occupied by someone else, you were never really gone. Your likeness would always be there.

Despite the fact that Walter's and Lucile's photos hung on the Wall of Residents, a gray cloud of sadness hung over our little village. The zest for life that usually characterizes our community was diminished just a little. Life demands to be lived, but sometimes the clouds of sorrow taint the joy just a bit. Since Walter and Lucile had been single and lived in singles apartments, two new people would be joining our family. They would be welcome, but they wouldn't be Walter and Lucile. It would take some time.

Cybil had given a couple of tours earlier in the day; each time it had been an older woman and two younger people, probably her grown children looking for a comfortable, happy place for Mom. When I was younger, I used to think it was awful that older parents with grown children had to go live in retirement homes. Old folk's homes. That's how I used to think of them. But now that I'm one of those older parents and live in one of those *homes*, I wouldn't have it any other way. David is a good son, and he's trying to be a good dad to Nikki. He has a comfortable home, and technically there is room for us there. But I would not want to live with David and Nikki. I love them, but live with them? No thanks. No way.

On Thursday, a new woman, Gwyneth Nichols, moved into Walter's old room on the second floor, just a few doors down from us. Cybil brought her around and introduced her to several people. She looked to be in her late seventies or early eighties. Sometimes it can be hard to tell. She was smallish and looked sad. Recently widowed, I suspected. But now was not the time to make inquiries. I made a mental note to give it a few weeks and then broach the subject.

Whenever someone new moved in, Cybil liked to assign them to someone who would serve as a mentor—someone to show them and introduce them around and help them get acclimated to our little community. Cybil assigned Elizabeth to help Gwyneth. A brilliant move, I thought, providing Gwyneth with the help she needed as well as giving Elizabeth someone other than Walter to think about.

At dinner that night, Frances Logan announced that they had another great granddaughter. This made three. Jennifer Logan Beal—six pounds, eight ounces—had been born just a few hours ago at two twenty-three in the afternoon. Everyone applauded. It made me smile. But it also made me a tad philosophical. Old people die; new ones are born to replace them. The circle of life goes on. Except in this case, the two people who died did so before their time. And that wasn't right. I was going to discover what happened. And if I could, I'd keep it from happening again.

Chapter 32

Harry and I left Happy Trails at seven to go visit Georgette and Oscar. The evening was clear and not too cool. Light sweater weather. Harry put a Beatles CD in the stereo, and as he pulled out onto Catclaw, said, "BettyJo's dream bothering you at all?"

"You mean that Georgette might still die?"

"That is what she said."

"I think BettyJo thinking her dreams are prognostications is a wagon load of road apples."

"I see," Harry said. "What about the fact that she had her dream about the death certificates the night before Walter died?"

"Coincidence."

"Coincidence," Harry said. "So her dream about Walter and Lucile dying in close proximity to their actual deaths is mere coincidence, but their deaths in close proximity are not."

"Do you believe in clairvoyance and ESP and all that stuff?" I asked.

"Most of the time people claim to know something or to have seen something or to sense something, it's a load of crap. They're either nut jobs or are lying—con artists and all that stuff. But there are some cases where people do genuinely seem to have known or perceived something, often before it happens, without the benefit of normal sensory input."

"And you think BettyJo's dreams might be that?"

"I don't know," he said. "I just wondered what you thought."

"Road apples."

"Don't beat around the bush. What do you really think?

Georgette was awake and talking when we walked into her room. She had partial vision in her left eye, but there was some double vision as well. She seemed to be in good spirits, though, and so did Oscar. I was relieved. I'd have to be sure to tell BettyJo that Georgette was recovering nicely.

We got back to Happy Trails a little before eight and went to the cafeteria for some no sugar added apple or cherry pie and some decaf coffee. Why is it that in order to enjoy the wisdom that comes with age, you have to give up the pleasures of sugar and caffeine?

As we ate our pie and coffee, Harry said, "If you think about the fact that there's no sugar added in the pie and they've taken the caffeine out of the coffee, you feel kind of cheated."

"So don't think about it," I said.

"Exactly," Harry said. "It becomes a metaphor for life. The longer you live the less you can enjoy the sugar and the caffeine."

"And the analogy is …?"

"You just have to take what life hands you, not think too much about it, and … eat it."

"I love it when you get all philosophical," I said.

We sat and visited with friends for a while and went up to our room a few minutes before ten. Harry turned on the news and picked up his book. I used my phone to check my email, deleted the junk, and read what was left, which wasn't much. I clicked on the Facebook icon and while it opened, looked up at the TV. They were doing a story about a big pharmaceutical company in Dallas, AFO, that just bought out a competitor and was now the largest pharmaceutical company in the country. With the new acquisition, its value was now estimated to be right at sixty billion dollars. Lots of money in pharmaceuticals, I thought. Then, in a related story, they talked about a bill in Congress that would streamline the drug approval process. They ran a video of an attractive young woman, a vice president of a much smaller pharmaceutical company explaining that one of the reasons drug prices were so high was the amount of time and money it took to get the FDA to approve a new drug. Streamlining the approval process, the woman explained, would result in lower prices at the retail end of the pharmacy process.

"That would be nice," I said to Harry.

"What?" he said, looking up from his book.

"The price of prescriptions meds going down," I said.

"Another politician promising to do something about that?"

"Not a politician. A pharmaceutical executive. There's a new bill before Congress."

"Uh-huh."

139

"But the other side of the argument," I said, "is the assured safety of medications. Without extensive testing, how can the FDA be sure a drug is safe?"

"It's a conundrum."

"I remember once years ago a new medication for acne came out. Supposed to clear it right up. And it did. Worked like a charm. The stuff was flying off the shelves. Every teenager in the country was buying the stuff. The problem was that about fifteen percent of people who used it, developed a severe eye twitch and swelling of the tongue."

"Let me guess," Harry said, "the instructions didn't specifically say they weren't supposed to put it in their eye or on their tongue."

"You may be on to something. It was, after all, a product for teenagers. But as the chemicals in it got absorbed through the skin and into the bloodstream, it caused undesirable side effects in fifteen percent of users."

"And the tests they did before the product was approved didn't reveal the possibility of serious adverse side effects?" Harry asked.

"They probably did. I suspect no one paid attention. Or the possibility of the problematic side effects was not adequately communicated."

"Why do the testing if you're not going to publish the findings so people know the risks?"

"Exactly," I said. "So streamlining the approval process is not the solution. That will just make the existing problem worse."

"So what's the answer?" Harry asked.

"A lower profit margin."

Chapter 33

Friday morning as Harry and I were finishing our breakfast, Linda came to our table looking distressed. "I need a favor," she said, sitting down next to me.

"Sure," I said. "What do you need?"

"My mother had a stroke last night."

"I'm so sorry. How bad was it?"

"Could have been worse, but right now she's paralyzed on her right side and can't talk. Dad didn't call last night because he didn't want to bother me."

"He's ninety and has trouble getting around. Uses a walker. Mom's eighty-seven. And they still live alone. I've got to go help out. I've told Cybil, and she called the temp agency, but they won't have anyone available until Tuesday. We need someone to fill in for me until then. Since you've kept your license active, you seemed like the logical choice. Cybil said if you were willing she was okay with it."

"Be glad to do whatever I can."

"Oh, thank you. You're a lifesaver. Listen, I hate to rush your breakfast, but I need to get on the road."

141

"They live in Dallas, right?"

She nodded. "Two and a half hours to their house. Another ten minutes to the hospital."

"Okay. Let's go to your office." To Harry I said, "Sorry. Duty calls."

"I'll check in on you later," he said.

We went to Linda's office, which was next door to Cybil's. "Okay," Linda said as soon as the door closed behind us. "It's really not all that complicated. You probably know all this already, but let me do a quick run through. First, everything's in the computer. Each resident has a file— general medical history, allergies, concerns of any kind, medications prescribed, special nutritional needs, if any. All that sort of stuff. Some of the residents need help with their medications, most don't. But all the medications are delivered here. They're purchased through mail order and come to the patient in care of Happy Trails. We check all the labels against what's in the computer to make sure each resident is getting the correct medication in the correct dosage. If they are and that resident does not require special assistance, we pass the medication on to the resident, and they take it themselves. If they need assistance, we hold the medications and Jenny and Ellie make their rounds each day, making sure those who need help get and take their meds. Not a lot for you to do there. Jenny and Ellie are very efficient."

She was right. I already knew how the system worked, so I just listened and nodded.

"What I'm most concerned about is if there is an accident or an emergency of some sort. You'll be the first responder until the EMTs arrive. Of course, you have to decide whether or not it's something you can and should handle with basic medical, which is usually a bandage or an aspirin, or if you need to call 911—like if someone falls and breaks a hip or something."

"Got it," I said.

"Jenny's already here," Linda added, "and is handing out meds. She's day shift. Twelve hours. Ellie is night shift. She comes in at six."

"Is there a password for the computer?" I asked.

"Yeah. Good thing you asked. It's, letsplaydoctor. All lower case, no spaces."

"Cute."

"No one else has the password. Those files are absolutely confidential."

"Don't Jenny and Ellie need access?"

"No. I've prepared a matrix with all the information they need to assist with medication. It's on the wall in the storage room through that door. Have you ever been in there?"

"No."

"Let me show you."

Her desk sat in the middle of the room. In the wall to her right as she sat at her desk was a door that led into a room almost as large as her office. It was filled with medical equipment and supplies, including locked cabinets filled with residents' medications. Mine and Harry's was in there somewhere. We got ninety days worth at a time. Linda put a thirty-day supply in our mailbox each month. Efficient.

"Here are the keys to my office, to this room, and to the medical cabinets."

I took the keys.

She looked around nervously. "I think that's all. Oh, no, wait." She went to her desk and picked up a cell phone. "This is the nurse's phone. Everybody here has this phone number. If they need something, they'll call this phone. So you need to keep it with you all the time."

"I will. Don't worry."

Linda looked stressed.

"Everything will be fine, Linda. Go help your parents."

As Linda turned to leave, I said, "Drive carefully. Don't rush." She was out the door. "And be careful of those drivers in Dallas," I added. "Those people are nuts." I don't think she heard me.

As I was sitting down at Linda's desk, Cybil came in. "I wanted to thank you for filling in."

"Glad to help."

"I'll pay you what I would have paid the temp."

"No need to pay me."

"Yes, there is. You work, you should get paid. And you don't need to sit here in the office all day. As long as you've got the phone and you're reasonably nearby, you'll be fine. So go on about your day."

I thanked Cybil, and she left. I looked at the computer screen. Okay, I said to myself, what to do first? Like that was a difficult decision. I searched for Walter's file and started going through it. After all, I was officially the Happy Trails nurse and as such had legitimate access to resident medical records.

I read every bit of Walter's medical file. He was as healthy as a man of eighty could be. In fact, he was in better shape than a lot of men twenty years younger. And there was absolutely no reason for him to have a heart attack. I went to Lucile's file and read it. She also appeared to be perfectly healthy for a woman of her age. There was nothing in her file that would have made anyone think she was a candidate for a brain tumor. Neither was Georgette. Her file indicated that she, too, was in good shape. So what had happened?

While I was ruminating on the possibilities, Jenny came in. "Hi, Harriet," she said. "Linda said she was going to ask you to fill in for her until the temp agency could send someone over. Too bad about her mom. I hope she's okay."

"Me, too."

"Well, if you need anything, just holler."

"There is something I'd like to ask you."

"Sure."

"Prescription medicine is sent here and passed on to residents. But what if someone just found something they wanted to take. Found it in a pharmacy somewhere or ordered it online. Is there any way to monitor that?"

"Not that I can think of."

"Me, either. But I just wanted to ask."

"You think that Walter, Lucile, and Georgette were taking something non-prescription?"

"Unless what happened to them was just coincidence, it's the only thing that makes any sense."

"Could be, I guess."

"Has anyone said anything to you about taking any new medications?"

She shook her head. "Not to me. You should ask Ellie when she comes on tonight."

145

Chapter 34

Jenny went to check the mail and log in any medications that had arrived. As I sat thinking, Nikki called.

"It's a school day," I said. "Why aren't you in school?"

"I took the day off."

"Why?"

"Because I'm upset. It's a mental health day."

"Uh-huh. What are you upset about?"

"Dad and I talked last night. He says part of why he's depressed, I mean other than Mom leaving, is because he hates his job. He doesn't want to be a mechanic anymore."

"Does he know what he wants to do?"

"Yeah. He wants to be a cop, like Grandpa was."

"And?"

"And I don't want him to be a cop. But I didn't tell him. I wanted to talk to you first."

"Why don't you want him to be a cop?"

"Because cops get killed. You hear it on the news all the time."

I understood what she was feeling. "Okay," I said, "here's what we're going to do. I'm going to send Grandpa over to get you. While he's on his way, you call your Dad and tell him that you stayed home from school because you really needed to talk to me about some stuff. Tell him I said it was okay because you and I need some girl time. Will you do that?"

"What if he asks me what I'm upset about?"

"Tell him it's girl stuff and you don't want to talk to him about it, you want to talk to me. Will you do that? Will you call him?"

"Okay."

"All right. Grandpa will be on his way in just a bit."

I called Harry's cell and caught him just before he went for his morning swim. I explained, and he said he'd leave in just a minute.

"Do you think you need to talk to David?" I asked. What I meant was, *you need to talk to David.* But I hated being that direct. It felt too bossy. It had taken me years to train Harry to understand indirect communication. The problem was that even though he understood what I was saying, he didn't always agree.

"No."

"Why not?"

"Because he's a grown man. I can't treat him as if he were a kid. If he wants to talk to me, we'll talk. I'll tell him what I think. But he has to come to me. I can't presume and go to him."

It didn't sound to me like the right approach.

Sensing that I was not convinced, he said, "Harriet, this is a guy thing. I have to respect him. Let it be."

147

"Fine. But you can talk to me about it, right?"

"Yes, I can talk with you."

I could hear the smile in his voice.

"What is it you want to talk about?" he asked.

"He's depressed. Got PTSD. Should he be carrying a gun?"

"Hon," Harry said softly, "he already carries a gun. Besides, cops get depressed just like everyone else. You know that. Doesn't mean they can't do their job. Some of the surgeons you worked with were probably depressed while they were doing surgery. No one told them they couldn't use a scalpel. Besides, David's PTSD isn't so bad that he can't manage it. He gets up each day and goes to work and does his job just like I did when I got back from Nam."

"Yeah, okay. I guess."

"You were a cop's wife for a long time. I can't think of anyone better to help Nikki work through her concerns about her Dad being a cop."

Harry hung up and left to get Nikki. I sat for a while and remembered what it was like when Harry was working. He knew I worried about him. But I don't think he understood how much I worried, how often I prayed for his safety, and how often I jumped when the phone rang, worried that it was a call to tell me he'd been shot. Being a cop's wife, even in a small, relatively safe town like Abilene, was no piece of cake. What was I going to tell Nikki about being the daughter of a cop?

Of course, this was all contingent upon David getting the job. Maybe he wouldn't. Oh, who was I kidding? David was just the kind of candidate they were looking for. Former military. Infantry. From a cop family. Big, like his dad.

Smart, dedicated, tough. Every cop in Abilene knew Harry, and most of the older ones would remember David from when he was a teenager. If he applied for a job with the Abilene Police Department, he'd get it.

Chapter 35

I wanted to check the medications that were listed in the computer with what was actually sitting on the shelves in the secure storage room. I figured I'd have time before Harry showed up with Nikki. I was nearly done, happy that so far everything on the shelves was listed in the computer, when Harry and Nikki arrived.

"Wow," Nikki said. "Old people take a lot of drugs, don't they?"

"Hey," I said. "Be careful about how you use the word *old* when you're in a retirement village."

"You mean like old people live in an old folks home?" she said mischievously.

"Exactly," Harry said. "You talk like that and the retirement police will come to your house and take away your X-Box or your Game Boy, or your boy toy or whatever it is."

That made her laugh.

"I'm almost done here," I said. "Why don't the two of you go get a cup of coffee and I'll be along in a few minutes."

Most of what was on the shelves was basic stuff: different pain medications, meds for blood pressure, cholesterol, blood sugar, and so forth. Nothing that was odd or out of place for the group of people that lived at Happy Trails. I was both relieved and frustrated. Part of me was hoping to find something that might have caused a heart attack or a brain tumor. I suppose that would have been too easy. And it would have meant that Linda was, at least to some degree, complicit in their deaths. I was glad that was not the case.

Harry and Nikki were sitting in the back of the cafeteria drinking coffee and talking. I got myself a cup of coffee and joined them. Harry was saying, "Most of the time police work is asking a lot of questions and filling out a lot of forms and writing reports. It's actually pretty boring. There are cops all across the country who never have to pull their weapon even once in their entire career. The few cops who get shot each year make up only a small percentage of the police officers across the country. Then there's the fact that Abilene is a small town. There's not a lot of violent crime here. Since 2010 there have been six line of duty deaths in the APD, and only three of those were shootings. It's not like cops in Abilene are getting shot at every day."

Nikki looked at me. "Did you worry about him?"

"Of course I did. I worried every day. But you learn to live with it. It was his job and he loved doing it. And he was good at it."

I could see that she still wasn't fully convinced.

151

"It was a team effort," I said. "His job was doing the job; my job was worrying about him and encouraging him. Between us, we got the job done."

"Did you know," Nikki asked Harry, "that she was worried about you?"

"Sure I did."

"And you let her worry."

Harry smiled. "Being a police officer is important work. Somebody has to do it. It's crucial that we have good men and women upholding our laws and protecting our citizens. It was the job I wanted to do. I knew your grandmother was strong enough to help me do it. She's right when she said it was a team effort."

"I guess I can understand that," Nikki said.

"Any other questions?" Harry asked Nikki.

"No. I get it. Thanks, Grandpa."

"You're welcome, Sweetie. Now, I've got other things I need to do, so I'll leave you girls to enjoy your time together." As he stood to leave he said, "If your dad decides to become a cop, he'll be a good one."

Nikki nodded and smiled.

"It's a nice day out," I said. "Want to go for a walk?"

"Sure."

I figured Harry wanted to get in his daily swim before lunch. So while he did that, Nikki and I headed out to the walking trail at the back of the main building that leads to the park on the south side of the golf course. There was a gentle breeze, but not enough to make it chilly. "There's something else I want you to think about," I said.

"What?"

"Your mom's been gone for what, a year now?"

"Yeah."

"At some point your dad's probably going to start dating again. When he does, you need to be supportive."

"I know. I thought about that. Things are just so messed up right now. I'm really worried about his PTSD. I mean, you hear all kinds of stories about guys that are really messed up."

"I know. And that can be scary. But in the past few months I've been reading up on it. Think of it like this. Lot's of people are overweight. Some people are five or ten pounds overweight, some are twenty or thirty or fifty pounds overweight, and then there are the seriously overweight people. Obese people who are three or four hundred pounds overweight. It's not good to be overweight. But five or ten pounds overweight, or even fifteen or twenty, is not that dangerous. PTSD is kind of like being overweight. There are different degrees of PTSD. You dad's PTSD is not super serious. It's not debilitating. He has bad dreams; he's depressed sometimes. But he's managing it, and he's living life. And it's not just the PTSD that causing the problems. Some of it is your mom leaving, and him not being happy in his job. Maybe getting a new job will help."

"I guess," Nikki said. "And maybe if he meets someone nice and starts dating, that will help."

"It might. And when he does bring someone home to meet you, you need to be supportive. Whoever she is, she won't be trying to replace your mom."

Nikki blew out a puff of air and said, "Mom needs to be replaced. The dumb bitch."

"Nikki!"

153

"Well, she does need to be replaced. She was mean to dad. She hurt him for no reason."

"You don't really know exactly what happened between them, do you?"

"No."

"And you're still struggling with it, too, aren't you?"

"Yes," she said, anger in her face as well as her voice. "She screwed up our family."

"I know. And there's nothing you and your dad can do about it but be supportive of each other."

We had reached the little lake and had gone out onto the bridge. We stopped and leaned against the rail. The koi came looking for food. Nikki took a deep breath. "I understand what you're saying, Grandma. And I'll try to be supportive of Dad. For his job and when he brings a girlfriend home."

I smiled at her.

"You think he'll be supportive of me when I bring my boyfriend home?"

"That will probably depend on the young man you bring home. Fathers are very protective of their daughters."

I put a quarter in the machine and got some pellets to feed the fish. I gave most of them to Nikki. We fed the fish in silence for a few moments. Then I said, "Nikki, being a girl and being a young woman are not the same things. Because of the way things have worked out, life may not seem fair right now. But that's the way life is sometimes. You may have to put on your big girl panties sooner than you might otherwise have needed to. And I'm not talking about shopping for underwear at Victoria Secret."

Nikki smiled. "I understand."

We finished feeding the fish and started back.

"Grandma."

"Yes?"

"Some aspects of growing up suck."

"Yes, they do."

Chapter 36

Nikki stayed through lunch and then Harry drove her back home. I went back to the nurse's office to look around some more. Jenny reported that everyone who needed help with their medication had taken what they were supposed to take and were happy. Out of the seventy-five residents, only twelve currently needed assistance with medication, so it wasn't a big job.

Jenny also taught the afternoon exercise class, so while she went off to do that, I thought I'd do a little more research on drugs that could generate serious negative side effects. Turns out there are a ton of them. Most of them are safe for most people. But some of them can be dangerous for a small group of people. The challenge was trying to figure which drug would cause problems in which people. There was a Noble prize waiting for me if I figured that one out.

I'd been looking for information about problematic drugs for about twenty minutes when Kramer came in—his large nose arriving a couple of seconds before the rest of him.

"Hi, Kramer. What can I do for you?"

"Where's Linda?" he asked, studying me with his beady little eyes.

I noticed his nose hair needing trimming. "Her mother is ill," I said. "She had to take some time off to help out."

"Oh. That's too bad. But you're a nurse, too, so I guess it's okay."

I smiled, convinced that Kramer couldn't help it. "How can I help you?"

"I got a date tonight with a hottie from the Oak Grove Retirement Home, and I need some little blue pills."

"Do you have a prescription for Viagra?"

"Not that I know of. Never needed it before. The thing is, it's been a while since I been out with a woman, and I want to be prepared."

"I see. Always good to be prepared. The problem is, Viagra is a prescription medication. A doctor has to write you a prescription for it. I can't just give it to you."

"I only need a half dozen or so."

At least he was optimistic.

"Sure. But even if it was just one, which I assure you would be more than adequate, I couldn't give it to you."

"Charlie's got a prescription for it. Give me a couple of his. He won't miss them."

"Kramer, I can't give you someone else's medication. Why don't you just take Ms. Hottie to dinner and then go see a movie."

"What kind of a date would that be?"

Frankly, I couldn't imagine a woman actually wanting to have sex with Kramer unless she was desperate, but I was trying to be nice.

157

"It might be a very nice date. You could enjoy some nice conversation."

Kramer looked at me as if I had a monkey sitting on my head.

"Talking with her," he said, as if the idea were strange. "I never thought of that. What would we talk about?"

"I don't know. What kinds of things is she interested in?"

"What I heard," he said, "is she's interested in getting laid."

"Oh, for Pete's sake, Kramer. I don't have any Viagra to give you. Go away."

He pulled back slightly as he took in some air, turned, and went to the door. Before leaving, he said, "When Linda gets back I'm gonna tell her you were mean to me."

"Get."

He left. I think I scared him. Good. Poor woman.

I went back to the computer, and ten minutes later Mrs. Peltzer came in. "Hi, Agnes. How can I help you?"

She didn't look good.

"I'm not feeling well. I don't know what's wrong."

"What are your symptoms?"

"My heart is racing, I'm sweating, I have pain in my stomach and I feel light-headed."

"When did this start?"

"Just a little while ago."

"Did anything happen to upset you before the symptoms appeared?"

"I don't think so."

I grabbed the stethoscope and listened to her heart pounding away in her chest. I timed her pulse. It was eighty-seven. I took her blood pressure. 152 over 94. Way too high.

"Did you take your blood pressure medication this morning?"

"Yes."

"Did you take anything new?"

"Well, the doctor just put me on metformin for my blood sugar a few days ago."

"Metformin, huh. I suspect that's what's causing this."

"He told me it would give me diarrhea for a while until my system got use to it. But he didn't say anything about all this other stuff."

"It doesn't cause these side effects in everyone. That's probably why he didn't mention them."

"What should I do? I feel terrible."

"Was it Dr. Bascom?"

"Yes."

"Okay, you need to call him and let him know and schedule an appointment to see him. Or I can call and schedule something for you."

"No, I can call him. Thank you. I appreciate it."

The rest of the day was quiet. I spent a total of two hours looking for drugs that were known to cause heart attacks and brain tumors. There were some medications that might cause heart problems in some people, and some different medications that might cause brain tumors in some patients. I couldn't find a drug that might cause either heart problems or brain tumors. What were the odds that three people at the same retirement village would be taking different medications that caused such severe side effects? They had to be astronomical.

When I got tired of thinking, I put the nurse's phone in my pocket, and even though it was approaching my afternoon caffeine cut-off time, I headed to the self-serve coffee and tea station in the cafeteria. If I drink caffeine too late in the day, I lay awake half the night berating myself for enjoying a shot of caffeine so late in the afternoon. But if I hurried, I had time. I got myself a cup of real coffee and went out onto the patio to sit in the sun. A chilly breeze had begun to blow, however, so that didn't last long. I took my coffee and went to the ceramics room to work on the project I'd been neglecting—a copy of a Grecian urn I'd seen in a history book. I'd shaped it on the wheel, fired it, and glazed it. Now I needed to paint it. I knew what I wanted to paint— a picture of the acropolis from a distance—but I just couldn't get motivated. I couldn't get my mind, tired or not, off the deaths of two of my friends. At least Georgette had survived.

Chapter 37

Usually we go out for something to eat after church. This time, since Alice was serving chicken and dumplings, Harry's favorite, we decided to eat lunch at Happy Trails. It was quarter to twelve as we walked into the dining room and got in line.

We sat down at a table for four and in a moment were joined by Ed and Jimmy who regaled us with their adventures in Sunday morning golf. Apparently Ed and Jimmy beat their rivals, Frank and Bob, by two strokes thanks to the three birdies made by Jimmy.

"It was a glorious thing to behold," Ed said.

I got the feeling that they would be telling the story to anyone who would listen for several days.

The meal was winding down, and a few people had already made their way to the dessert section of the buffet when Cybil stood to speak. When everyone had given her their attention, she said, "I'm sorry to have to tell you that this morning at eleven fourteen Georgette passed away."

Several people gasped, but otherwise there was stunned silence. She had come through the surgery and was recovering nicely. What had happened?

"A few minutes before eleven, while talking to Oscar she suddenly had a seizure. A few minutes later, she was dead. The doctor is at a loss to explain what happened. The tumor that had impacted her optic nerve was successfully removed. Perhaps there was another tumor that the MRI did not pickup or the doctor missed when he looked at the scan. Either way, we've lost another friend. I returned with Oscar just a while ago. He's in his room right now trying to pull himself together. We'll keep you updated as more information becomes available."

"What's going on?" Jimmy asked after a moment. "Everybody's dying."

"I don't know," I said.

"There's something not right about it," Jimmy said. "Up until a couple of weeks ago everything was fine. Now people are dropping like flies. You think something's going on here that God don't like, and he's punishing the evil doers?"

"Knock it off, Jimmy," Ed said. "God isn't punishing anyone for anything."

"How do you know? Walter was having sex with any woman who'd let him."

"God doesn't kill people for having sex. Besides, Lucile and Georgette weren't part of Walter's harem, were they?"

Jimmy looked deflated. "No, I suppose not. But how do you explain it?"

"I can't," Ed said.

"Harriet," Jimmy said, "how do you explain it?"

"I can't, either. At least, not yet."

No one felt like doing much of anything Sunday afternoon. At three, Harry and I went to see if Oscar felt like talking. We took three coffees with us.

"Come in," he said. His eyes were red and puffy.

"Brought you some coffee," Harry said after Oscar had closed the door.

"What can we do to help?" Harry asked.

Oscar shook his head. "I'd like for you to be one of the pallbearers. Other than that, I don't think there's anything anyone can do. Our son will be coming from Houston. He'll help me with all the arrangements."

We sat with him a while. He cried; we cried. There wasn't much to say.

After a while, Harry signaled to me that we should go. I nodded. "If there's anything you need," I said, "just ask."

"I know. Thank you."

Alice had put out extra desserts, knowing that people would want to sit and talk. A lot of the talk was about what was going on. Three deaths in just over two weeks. As Harry and I visited with Elizabeth and Julie, Diane came over and sat down. Diane had come to Happy Trails almost two years ago just after her husband died. Her daughter who lives in Sweetwater wanted her to come live with her and her family, but Diane wanted to stay in Abilene and continue to be active in her church.

"I was just on the phone with my daughter, Kerri."

"The one in Sweetwater?"

"Yes. And she told me that this morning in church they announced that one of the ladies there who lives in the

163

Elm Creek Assisted Living Community died of a heart attack. She said it was a complete shock to everyone because this woman, Noelle Green, seemed to be so healthy."

"I'm sorry to hear that," I said. "How old was she?"

"Early eighties, I think. Look, I don't know what's going on, but this all seems odd to me. Too many healthy people dying all of sudden. I know you're concerned, too, because you've been asking around about medications. Anyway, I just wanted you to know that Happy Trails isn't the only place where this is happening."

When Harry and I went back to our room, I got online and looked up deaths in Texas retirement homes in March 2019. Besides the ones I knew about, there had been two others. One was in the Livingstone Assisted Living Community in Fort Worth, and one in Countryside Retirement Village in Cisco. The man in Fort Worth had died of a heart attack; the woman in Cisco had died of a brain tumor.

Chapter 38

It was Thursday morning, and the temp agency still hadn't sent anyone to fill in for Linda, so I was still the acting nurse. There hadn't been any emergencies, and Jenny and Ellie did most of the real work to be done. I didn't know how much Linda made as the Happy Trails nurse, but it didn't seem like she worked very hard for it. I would not have wanted the job on a full time basis. Not enough to do. I'd get bored. I'd take Harry out for a fancy dinner when I got paid.

Georgette's funeral was at ten. She and Oscar had been active in a big church here in town, and the funeral was going to be held there. At eight twenty, I knocked on Cybil's door and stuck my head in her office. "Got a minute?"

"Sure. Come in."

I went in and sat down in one of the guest chairs in front of her desk. "Still no word from the temp agency?"

"No. And things have been pretty quiet, as they usually are, so I haven't made a real effort to get someone. Have you had enough?"

165

"No, it's not that. But I do need some time to take care of some business."

"Go ahead. No problem. Jenny's here. Just keep the nurse's phone with you. If there's something big, we'll call you. Otherwise, go do what you need to do."

"Okay. It'll be this afternoon, after Georgette's funeral. And maybe some tomorrow as well. Depends on how things go."

"No problem," Cybil said.

The pastor at Georgette's and Oscar's church was a young man in his early forties. His message was very hopeful, and the singing, which was all *a cappella,* was absolutely beautiful. It was a very nice service.

From the church, we went to the cemetery for a brief graveside service. The graveside service is the hardest part for me—the casket sitting over the open grave, the mound of dirt next to it. The idea of the casket being lowered into the ground, covered with dirt. The cold, loneliness of it all. I knew Georgette wasn't in the casket. She was with Jesus. Only her body was in the casket. But that body had been part of who she was. And now it was being put into the ground to decay. If I weren't a Christian, life would seem rather pointless. Futile.

On the way home, I told Harry about the deaths in Sweetwater and Cisco.

"And you don't think they're a coincidence," he said.

"Do you?"

"Old people die," Harry said. "They die of heart attacks. Some of them die from brain tumors. But given the number of apparently healthy people who have died recently in retirement homes of heart attacks and brain tumors, I'd say, no, we're not dealing with coincidence here."

"What should we do?"

He took a deep breath and blew it out. "There still isn't actual evidence of wrongdoing. There's nothing to take to the police. So basically you need to keep looking. You need something to give to the police, some piece of evidence that points to something more than coincidence."

"Maybe we need to go to Sweetwater and Cisco and talk to the people there. Maybe there's family in the area that we can talk to."

"Yeah," Harry said. "I think that's a good idea."

We went back to Happy Trails, changed into more casual clothes, and spent time talking about the funeral. We looked for Oscar to see how he was doing. His children, two sons and a daughter, were with him, all of them looking numb from the morning's sad experience. We ate lunch, and at one thirty, we headed out to the small town of Cisco, forty-five minutes east of Abilene.

Generally speaking, as you drive east across the northern half of Texas toward the Dallas-Fort Worth metroplex and beyond, the terrain changes, becomes greener, more lush. But the drive from Abilene to Cisco doesn't take you far enough east for there to be any difference in the way things look. The terrain remains the same: a few small, rolling hills with short scrub oak and bent mesquite trees scattered across the dry, reddish brown soil. If you like that sort of thing, the drive can be pleasant. Fortunately, having grown up here, I like it. The drive was relaxing.

We found Countryside Retirement Village on the north side of town, on the road out to Lake Cisco. It looked like a nice little community. All the buildings were single-story red brick of similar design but different sizes. A large square building with white pillars dominated the front of the complex. The administration building, no doubt, and probably the cafeteria and community rooms, exercise room, and so forth. The small units behind it were apparently duplex cottages where the residents lived. There was a golf cart sitting in front of each residence, and wide covered walkways that connected the cottages and the main building. Beyond the buildings was a pool, and beyond that a golf course. Trees, shrubs and a well-manicured lawn softened the desert landscape, creating an appealing atmosphere. Nice.

Harry parked, and we went into the administration building. A pleasant-looking fifty-something woman appeared to be in charge of the front desk. I asked if we could see the administrator, and she said, "I don't see why not. Have a seat over there and I'll let her know you are here."

I suspected she thought we were potential customers. There didn't seem to be any point in bursting her bubble. In a moment, an efficient and sturdy-looking woman came out of a door behind the reception desk. "I'm Mrs. Hector. How can I help you?"

"I'm Harriet Ward and his is my husband, Harry. We live at the Happy Trails Retirement Village in Abilene, where I am currently the acting resident nurse. We were hoping you might be able to give us some information. Is there a place we can talk?"

"Certainly. Follow me."

She led us into her office, closed the door, and invited us sit in her guest chairs.

"Would you like some coffee?" she asked.

"Coffee would be good."

She picked up her phone, punched in a four-digit extension and asked for coffee for three.

"Now, how can I help you?"

I explained to her about the three deaths at Happy Trails, how their deaths seemed somewhat suspicious, and the scenario I was considering. Just as I finished my story, our coffee was delivered by the woman from the front desk. We paused to taste it—strong enough to get up and walk away if it had a mind to.

"So when I heard of the passing of Mrs. Winchester," I said, picking up where'd I left off, "I wondered if the circumstances were similar."

"Are the police involved in this matter?" Mrs. Hector asked.

"No, not at this time. But depending on what we find, they might be."

"Then I'm sorry. But I can't discuss the matter with you. Being a nurse, I'm sure you understand the confidentiality concerns involved."

"I do. But I'm not asking for confidential information, and Mrs. Winchester is dead. She no longer has concerns regarding confidentiality." I knew that wasn't true when I said it, but I figured it was worth a try.

"Even if Gladys doesn't," Mrs. Hector said, "her family does. I cannot discuss the matter with you."

She was right, but in a very annoying manner. I thanked her and we left. Once we were in the car, I said, "I'm thirsty. Can you find a convenience store?"

Harry found a 7-11 and went in to buy two Coke Zeros. While he was doing that, I looked up the obituary of

169

Gladys Winchester. She had a daughter, Judy Pearson, who lived right there in Cisco. I did a search for Judy Pearson and found an address. It is amazing what you can find online.

We drove to the Pearson home and went together to the door. A nice-looking middle-aged woman answered the door and turned out to be Judy Pearson. I explained, as I had to Mrs. Hector, about the deaths at Happy Trails and my concern that something other than coincidence might be involved. She listened patiently and seemed concerned. "Would you like to come in?"

"Yes. Thank you."

She had us sit and offered coffee. Harry said that coffee would be very nice. He had told me years ago that when he was questioning or interviewing witnesses in their homes, if they offered coffee, he always accepted it, even if he didn't really want any, because it helped to relax them and made them feel like they had nothing to fear by cooperating.

When she had served the coffee, Judy said, "Okay, so tell me again what has happened, and how you think it might involve Mom."

I began at the beginning and told her the story in detail—Walter's heart attack in spite of his good health, Lucile's and Georgette's brain tumors in spite of their good health, the time frame, and the additional retirement home deaths involving heart attacks and brain tumors.

By the time I was finished, Judy looked distressed. "Well, Mom's brain tumor took everyone by surprise because she also, like the people you described, appeared to be in good health."

"That's one of the factors that make us suspicious," I said.

"So, if I understand you, you're wondering if Mom was taking any new medication."

"Yes."

"I don't know. I wish I did. Mom was always headstrong. She always did what she wanted to do regardless of who didn't like it. Drove Dad crazy. If she found something that she thought she ought to take, she'd take it. But if she was, she didn't tell me."

I gave Judy a card with my number on it and asked her to call if she thought of anything. She said she would.

Chapter 39

The drive back to Abilene and then on out to Sweetwater took and hour and twenty minutes. Given the Coke Zero and the coffee that Harry drank, we had to make two pit stops. Funny how old men and old women have different issues when it comes to that sort of thing.

The Elm Creek Assisted Living Community was on the south side of town on a lonely looking piece of land out away from other buildings. It looked nice, it just looked lonely sitting out all by itself. It was probably pleasant and quiet, though. Instead of red brick, it was covered with pinkish brown slabs of rock. In addition to lonely, it looked formidable.

We parked in a visitor's spot and went in. The administrator, Andy Richards, was a tall, lean man with fair skin, gray curly hair, and green eyes. I suspected that when he was younger his hair was blond. I introduced myself and Harry and asked if we could talk in private. He invited us into his office, and asked us to sit down, but did not offer coffee. Probably just as well. The afternoon was wearing on, and we'd had a lot of caffeine.

"How can I help you?" Andy asked.

It was the correct question to ask, but I didn't sense there was much sincerity behind it.

I told him the same story I'd told Mrs. Hector in Cisco, and his response, while basically the same as Mrs. Hector's had been, was just a tad insulting. He said, "If there was foul play, the police should be looking into it, not a Jessica Fletcher wannabe."

At that point, Harry stood, put his clinched fists down on Andy's desk, leaned across the desk toward the tall, skinny man, and said. "You apologize to my wife, or I'll drag you out of that chair and kick you all the way out into the parking lot."

Harry's getting old, but when he reaches deep, it's all still in there, the look in the eye, the tone of the voice, and that indefinable something that told people that they were very close to suffering something very unpleasant.

Andy swallowed, and said, "I'm sorry, Mrs. Ward. It's been kind of a rough day. That was uncalled for. I apologize."

Harry straightened up and said, "We'll be going now."

When we got back to the Suburban, I went online again and got the information we needed. Noelle Green was the woman who died. She had a daughter and son who both lived in Sweetwater.

"Let's try the daughter first," I said.

Kendra Williams lived a few miles away in a nice ranch-style home in a upper middle class neighborhood. We got a friendlier welcome from her than we did from Andy.

"They handled all that sort of thing at Elm Creek," she said. "The doctor would prescribe something, and they'd make sure she got it. If she was taking anything extra, she didn't tell me. But that doesn't mean she wasn't. Mom didn't feel the need to share a lot about herself with others. She was her own woman. If she came across something that she thought would be good for her, she'd take it." Tears filled her eyes. "I just hope that's not what happened. How awful if she thought what she was taking was good for her and it's what killed her."

"Yeah. That's why we're trying to figure out if that's what happened. If people are taking something that's harmful, they need to know it."

"I'm glad there's someone who cares enough to look into it," Kendra said.

The drive back to Abilene was just about forty minutes. "You know what I can't figure," Harry said as he drove, the Moody Blues playing softly on the stereo, "is how everybody got hold of whatever it was they were taking. I mean, unless someone gave it to them, what are the odds that different people in different retirement communities would end up taking the same stuff. I mean, unless they're advertising the stuff on TV or in a magazine or something, how are they getting hold of it?"

"Good question," I said. "And why are they taking it? Is it being marketed to them? Or recommended to them? Why would they take it in the first place? What did they think it was going to do for them?"

It started to rain. Harry turned the windshield wipers on.

"Hope it's not going to be another big one," I said.

"Check your weather app."

I got out my phone and clicked my weather app, and wondered how we ever lived without instant information. "Nope. Not a big one. Just some rain."

"That's a good question you asked about the marketing thing," Harry said. "If it turns out that they were all taking the same stuff, why were they taking it? How did they hear about it? And how did they get hold of it?"

"I don't know."

"While you've got your phone out," he said, "do a search on marketing medications to seniors. See what comes up."

A bunch of stuff came up. Articles about how marketing drugs to seniors was a huge deal now because the baby boomers were getting older and needing medications. Lots of money in pharmaceuticals. In fact, there was one article that offered advice on ten ways to market medications to seniors.

"So if we're now assuming," Harry said, "that you're right, even though we do not yet have evidence to prove it, that each of the victims were taking something that caused their deaths, the questions are: How did they hear about it? How'd they get hold of it? And what was it?"

Chapter 40

Friday morning when I walked into the nurse's office, Linda was sitting behind her desk. "Oh, hi. I didn't know you were back."

"Got back late last night."

"How's your mother?" I asked.

"Getting better. The stroke was a mild one. The doctor thinks in time she'll be able to move normally again. But for now she still needs help, and with Dad's mobility issues ..." She shook her head. "They shouldn't be living alone. But I have to work. And I live in a one-bedroom house. I literally don't have room for them."

"I'm sure they understand."

"They might. They say they do. But they're my parents. I should be taking care of them."

"Maybe they could come here," I said. "Talk to Cybil. Maybe she can do something."

"I hadn't thought of that. I looked for a place for them in Dallas, but the only places that have openings are crappy places where I wouldn't send an enemy to live, let alone my parents."

"So what did you do?"

"I found someone to come in for several hours a day and help them."

"That's just a temporary fix."

"I know. I've got to figure out something else."

"I really think you should talk to Cybil."

"Maybe you're right."

"You heard about Georgette?" I asked.

"Yeah. I'm sorry."

I nodded.

"Anything serious happen while I was gone?"

I told her about Kramer and Agnes.

"Kramer," she said, shaking her head. "Silly old man. Nothing worse than a horny hypochondriac."

That made me laugh, and Linda smiled. "I appreciate you filling in for me," she said.

"Happy to do it."

Harry had gone for his morning swim and would then go to his painting class. I went to work on my ceramics project but couldn't get motivated. I put it away and went for a walk through our park. Most people go to the exercise room and walk on the treadmills or ride the stationary bikes. The way I figure it, exercise should involve doing something enjoyable, even if it's just meandering through our park on the walking trail. I was hoping something about this medication thing would occur to me while I was walking, but it didn't.

At lunch, Harry and I sat at a big round table. Four other people joined us: James, a retired school principal, and

177

his wife Lucy, who had been a licensed marriage and family counselor, Edna, a widow whose husband left her several million dollars in rental property here in Abilene, and Rebecca Adams, who had been a Texas state representative.

"Making any progress in your investigation?" Lucy asked me.

"Not yet."

"What investigation?" Edna asked.

Lucy looked at her as if she had weeds growing out of her ears. "You must be the only one in the whole place who isn't aware that Harriet is convinced that the deaths of Walter, Lucile, and Georgette so close together were not a coincidence. She thinks they were taking something that killed them."

Edna's eyes got big. "Really. What were they taking?"

"I don't know if they were taking anything," I said. "That's why I've been asking. I'm trying to find out. And they weren't the only ones. There have been three other recent deaths in other retirement communities, healthy people who died unexpectedly from either heart attacks or brain tumors."

Rebecca said, "Six people in the past few weeks in four different retirement communities died from either a heart attack or a brain tumor."

It wasn't a question as much as a statement that needed to be considered.

"So far," I said. "It wouldn't surprise me if there weren't more."

"That's disconcerting," Rebecca said. "Do you agree?" she asked Harry. Since everybody knew he was a retired detective, they were always interested in his opinion on detective kinds of stuff.

"In the beginning I had my doubts," he said. "Sometimes what appears to be a coincidence is just that. But given all that's happened, the more I think Harriet is right."

Rebecca didn't say anything else, but she was thinking about it.

Edna, apparently remembering what she considered an oddity of equal importance said, "Did you hear about the woman who saw the face of Jesus in the tortilla she was making?"

No one said anything for a moment. Finally, Lucy said, "The face of Jesus on a tortilla."

"She was making a batch of tortillas," Edna said, "and had one in the skillet. When she turned it over, there was the face of Jesus. So she takes it and wraps it in foil and puts it in a plastic bag and puts that in a small box and writes a note and sends it to the Pope at the Vatican. But somehow it got in the wrong stack of mail and got opened and put in with the kitchen stuff. The Pope saw it and used it to make a taco. Can you believe it?"

"No," James said.

Ignoring him, Edna said, "The Pope ate the face of Jesus. Unbelievable."

"In the truest sense of the word," James said.

Lucy, evidently, wasn't ready to move on from the issue of all of the unexpected deaths. She said, "Do you think anyone here is in danger?"

"If they are taking medication that wasn't prescribed for them," I said, "they could be."

"Maybe you should make an announcement," Lucy said. "Make sure everyone knows."

Chapter 41

As we were getting up from the table, Rebecca said, "Can I talk to you?"

I looked at Harry. "I'll be upstairs," he said.

"I'll be along in a bit," I said.

Rebecca's apartment is on the third floor. We got into the elevator. Rebecca seemed tense. "The Pope ate the face of Jesus?" I said, trying to lighten the mood.

Rebecca smiled but didn't saying anything. Something was really troubling her.

We went into the apartment. When she had closed the door she said, "Please have a seat. I have something I need to show you."

I sat down, and she went into the bathroom. When she came back, she handed me a bottle of pills and a letter. I looked at the bottle. The label said Forever Young. I looked at the letter. Good paper. Nice letterhead. I read it.

Dear Ms. Adams,

You are among a select few who have been chosen to enjoy the opportunity of a lifetime. You have the privilege of trying our new life-changing, energizing, age-reversing miracle compound, Forever Young. It is a compound made from the root of the baobab tree that grows near the Zambezi River in Zimbabwe, Africa. African tribes have known about and used this age-reversing, life-extending compound for ages. Now, for the first time, this miracle compound is available to a select few people who can try it for free for six months. All we ask is that after the free trial period you complete the enclosed survey form, explaining what benefits you realized from using this amazing, life-extending compound, and return it in the envelope provided.

To thank you for your participation in this opportunity, we will send you a month's supply of Forever Young absolutely free each month for six months. Take one pill each day and be amazed at the results.

The only other thing we ask is that in order to protect the integrity of this private offer you keep your participation in this unique, once-in-a-lifetime opportunity completely private. Please do not tell anyone about this product or your participation in this study.

If you want to participate in this exciting opportunity, please return the enclosed card with your name on it so we will know to send you more Forever Young.

Yours Truly,
Michael Young
President, Forever Young, Inc.
Lincoln, NE 68501

I looked at the bottle of pills again, opened the bottle and smelled the pills. Nothing. I read the letter again. This was incredible.

"Did you take any of these?" I asked.

Sheepishly, Rebecca said, "Yes."

The look on my face must have told her what I was thinking.

"Look at me," she said, "I used to be pretty. I figured it was probably a scam of some sort. The pills were probably just sugar pills and were harmless. I thought they'd ask for money at some point. If the pills worked, I'd pay them. If they didn't, I'd just toss them and forget it."

"So you sent the little card back, and they sent you more pills."

"Yes."

"How many did you take?"

"Two months worth, and a few more. That's the third bottle."

"How did they arrive?"

"In the mail."

"Do you know whether or not anyone else got one?"

"I don't. I did what they asked and kept the whole thing to myself. I assume that if anyone else got them, they did the same. Most people our age are sticklers for following directions."

The bottle looked to be half full or a little more. "Would you mind if I took these? I'd like to get them analyzed. Find out what's really in them."

"You don't believe what the letter said?"

"No."

Rebecca was wringing her hands. She'd been standing the whole time. She sat down opposite me, leaned toward me and said, "Do you think I'm going to die?"

"I certainly hope not. Who's your doctor?"

"Dr. Bascom."

"If I were in your place, I'd schedule an appointment and get my blood work done. Full spectrum. Explain this to him and ask him to look for any possible imbalance."

She was nodding. "Okay. I can do that."

"At this point," I said, "I think we should keep this to ourselves. No point in scaring everyone if there's no need."

She nodded. "Okay."

"Can I take the letter with me as well?"

"Sure."

"When I know something, I'll let you know. Try not to worry."

Chapter 42

"And she was gullible enough to take the pills?" Harry asked incredulously.

"Don't think too harshly of her. You've seen the photos. You know what she used to look like. Time was not kind to her."

"I guess. So, what'd you tell her?"

"I told her she should get her blood work done to see if there are any abnormalities."

"Because Georgette's doctor mentioned that her blood work was all out of whack."

"Yes."

"Probably good for her to do that."

"And I was hoping you could call in a favor."

"You want me to ask someone to have the pills analyzed."

"Could you?"

"I can probably get Will to do it. I got his fanny out of the fire more than once. He owes me."

"How fast can he get it done?"

Harry smiled. "If we explain the whole case to him, and he thinks it merits a quick turnaround, he may be able to get it done quickly."

Harry called Will, his former partner that he had helped train, and explained that we had something that could be a key piece of evidence in three suspicious deaths. Will said he could meet us at three at the Starbucks on Buffalo Gap and Danville.

Harry made sure we were there a few minutes early so he could buy coffee and scones for three. We staked out a small table as far away from everyone else as we could get and sat down. Will was there right at three. I hadn't seen him in a long time, a couple of years maybe. The lines had carved deeper into his face and his hair was beginning to speckle with gray. But he still had a friendly smile and warm eyes. He and Harry had been partners for the last six years of Harry's time on the force. They were good friends.

He sat, and we spent a few minutes catching up while sampling the coffee and scones. Then, Will said, "So, tell me about these three suspicious deaths."

"Actually, it's six deaths," I said. Then I began at the beginning and explained about Walter, Lucile, Georgette, and the three other people at the other retirement homes. I emphasized how healthy they were, and explained about my theory that they were taking something that generated lethal side effects. Finally, I got to the part about Rebecca, though I didn't tell him her name. I showed him the letter.

When he'd read it, he looked at me and I handed him the bottle of pills. He opened the bottle and shook a few pills into his hand. He held them up to his nose and smelled them.

"Looks ordinary enough," he said. "And you think the people who died may have been taking this stuff."

"I do."

"But you're not sure."

"Not yet. But if you can find out what it is, I can keep asking around."

"Where'd you get this?" Will asked.

"From one of the residents at Happy Trails."

"And you don't want to give me her name yet."

"Not if I don't have to."

He looked at Harry. "At first," Harry said, "I thought it was just coincidence. Several old people died unexpectedly. But the more people die of the same stuff … one or two maybe. But six? I think she's on to something."

"Okay," Will said. "I'll get this to our lab and try to expedite it. Soon as I have something, I'll call you."

On the way back to Happy Trails, David called Harry's phone. Harry put the call on speaker and set the phone on the console between us.

"Hi, Dad," David said. "Got a minute?"

"Sure," Harry said. "We're in the car."

"I took the afternoon off and went and applied for a new job."

After a long pause, Harry said, "Are you going to tell us, or do you want us to guess?"

"I applied to the APD," David said. I could hear the smile in his voice.

""That's good, son," Harry said. "Being a cop's a good job."

"I used you as a reference. I hope that's okay."

"Of course it's okay. I'd have been upset if you hadn't. I just hope they don't ask about that incident with the armadillo and the glow-in-the-dark paint when you were fourteen."

"I'm pretty sure the only way they could know about that is if you told them."

"You're probably safe, then. It's too embarrassing a story to tell anyone."

"Uh-huh."

"Anything I can do to help?"

"Speed the process up some."

"I can do a lot of things. That isn't one of them. Just be patient."

"What do you think, Mom?"

"I think you'll be an excellent police officer. I'm very proud of you."

Chapter 43

After dinner, Harry suggested we go for a walk. Since it was a bit breezy out, we went up to our apartment and grabbed our light jackets. As we came down the stairs to the first floor, we had to walk past the executive offices to get to the hallway that led to the rear entrance and the path out to the golf course and walking trail. As we passed Cybil's office, Cybil and a nice looking young woman were coming out. Probably a daughter looking for a place for one or both of her parents to live. Adult children came in quite often for a tour of the facilities. Since most of them work, they often came after they got off work. If Cybil wasn't there to give a tour and answer questions, the assistant director, Esther Meer, would show them around.

Cybil was walking the woman toward the front entrance, so I assumed she been given a tour. As we passed each other in the open area in front of the office, she looked vaguely familiar. She'd probably been in before. Sometimes people come three of four times before making up their minds, whether for themselves or for their parents. Making a

189

commitment to live in a retirement community is a big decision. Not the sort of thing you do on a whim.

The air was still, and even though it was cool, it was obvious spring had arrived. The days would be getting warmer and soon Harry would be talking about going fishing. We have a twenty-foot pontoon boat that we keep at the Boatel—clever name—near Lake Fort Phantom. It's not a beautiful lake, but there's pretty good fishing there. Over the years, we've enjoyed lots of good times on that lake.

"Any expectations as to what the lab guys will find?" I asked as we walked.

"Expectations," Harry said. "Not really. I mean they could be sugar pills, right? A total scam."

"They could be, I suppose. But if they are, they couldn't have caused any of the stuff that's happened."

"Yeah," he said. "And that doesn't feel quite right, does it?"

"No, it doesn't."

"But until he gets back to us, we just have to wait."

"And hope no one else dies in the meantime."

We went back to the cafeteria, and while we were having some decaf coffee and some no sugar added apple pie, we heard that someone had set up a 42 tournament in the big community room. "You up for a couple of hours of 42?" Harry asked me. "Might help take your mind off things."

"Sure. Why not?"

When we finished our dessert, we moseyed on over to the community room. Several games were already under way. At some of the tables, the men were teamed up against the women. At others, couples, usually husbands and wives, teamed up to play other couples. Harry and I preferred to play as a team. We found a four-person table that was open and sat down knowing someone would join us before too long. In a moment Gene and Sara Simpson asked if they could join us. Gene and Sara were relatively new to our Happy Trails family, having only been there a few months. Gene had been a math professor and Sara a human resources manager. When they retired, they came to Abilene to be near their daughter, who taught sociology at Hardin Simmons University. Sara had been diagnosed with Parkinson's, and Gene felt the wise thing to do was get settled into a living situation where medical help would be available when it was needed. So far Sara was holding her own against the disease, but they both knew it was only a matter of time.

"We're just learning this game," Gene said, "so you need to take it easy on us."

After winning two games, I asked if they'd rather play Scrabble. Sara looked relieved and said she'd love to play Scrabble. Harry gave me one of his looks. I don't think either Gene or Sara saw it, but I knew Harry would have preferred to play 42. Harry has a great vocabulary, but has trouble spelling cat.

"But this is a 42 tournament," Harry said.

"I know," I said, "But we've already won two games and in the last six months we've won three tournaments. I'd rather play Scrabble."

Harry knew that wasn't entirely true. I love 42. He knew I was just being nice to Gene and Sara.

"Okay," he said. "But you need to explain to them that we play *phonetic* Scrabble, because some people have trouble spelling words correctly."

"Yes, dear," I said. "What Harry is trying hard not to say is that he is spelling challenged, so we let him spell his words phonetically."

As we played, Gene, Sara, and I racked up quite a few points. Harry struggled to keep up. "You play golf?" he asked Gene.

"I tried to learn the game when I was younger. I know which end of the club to hold, but getting the ball in the cup … Well, I'm better at 42, and you see how I struggle with that."

"That good, huh?"

Gene smiled.

"What do you do to stay busy?" Harry asked.

"Actually, I'm trying to learn to write."

"Really. What kind of writing?"

"Mysteries. I want to be a novelist."

"You don't say. I read mysteries all the time. Who's your favorite mystery writer?"

And there they went. It took us an hour and a half to finish our Scrabble game because they were talking about their favorite mystery writers and characters.

Sara won the Scrabble game. I came in second, just a few points behind. At nine thirty, we said good night.

Chapter 44

The next afternoon at two twenty, Will called Harry and said he had a lab report on the suspicious pills. "Where do you want to meet?" Harry asked.

"How about the Dunkin Donuts on 14th Street? Three thirty?"

"See you then," Harry said.

We got there early, and Harry bought coffee and donuts—cop food—for three, and we sat down.

Will came in wearing brown slacks and a light blue polo shirt, his Glock clearly visible on his right hip. No one cared. This is Texas. I suspected Harry and Will weren't the only ones in the place who were carrying.

Will sat down. "Cop food," he said. "My favorite."

Harry smiled. Will handed Harry the lab report. "How'd you get it done so fast?" Harry asked.

"One of the lab techs is dating my daughter," he said. "He figured to score some points with me by staying late and working on it on his own time."

Harry smiled and scanned the report. "As always," Harry said, "most of this I don't understand. But the summary say that the pills are a compound of natural and synthetic substances, most of which are completely harmless and useless. Some are simple vitamins—B complex, C and D3. Ginko. Some other stuff that is thought to be good for you. Those things can be helpful. But some of the stuff in these pills can, in some people, cause serious side effects."

He looked at me as he handed me the report.

I read it. After the summary, was a list of possible side effects that included heart attack and brain tumors.

"Is this stuff FDA approved?" Harry asked.

Will took a sip of his coffee and said, "No."

"So if Walter, Lucile, and Georgette were taking this stuff," I said, "it may be what killed them."

"I'm not a doctor," Will said, "but that's how it appears to me. You ready to give me the person's name yet."

I thought. "How about this? How about if we show this to her and ask her how she wants to proceed?"

"Why the hesitation?"

"She used to be … a prominent person. I'd rather let her decide how to proceed than me making the decision for her."

Will hesitated just a moment, then said, "Okay. Normally I wouldn't agree to that, but since you're family…" And he cut his eyes to Harry.

"Thanks, Will. You need this report back?"

"No. That's a copy. You can have it."

"Thank you."

Will nodded and then said, "I hear we have a new hot shot applicant."

Harry smiled. "He's a good man. I think he'll be a good cop."

"Me, too," he said. Then he looked at me. "You all right with David following in his old man's footsteps?"

"I was a cop's wife for forty years. I guess I can manage being a cop's mother."

Chapter 45

On the way back to Happy Trails, as I was thinking about Rebecca's position, I realized she might not be anxious to talk to the police.

"When you were trying to convince a reluctant witness to testify," I said to Harry, "what did you say?"

He looked at me. "You worried that Rebecca won't want to get involved?"

"If you were in her position, would you be?"

"She's no longer a political figure. She has nothing to lose."

"Maybe," I said. "But if I put myself in her place, I can understand her reticence. What was your reaction when I told you she had taken the pills?"

He took a moment. "I asked you if she was gullible enough to take the pills."

"Exactly. And you're a friend."

"All right," he said. "I see your point. So you're asking me how I would try to convince her to cooperate with the police."

"Yes."

"When I had someone who was hesitant to get involved or testify, I would appeal to their sense of justice, assuming they had one, and I would talk about their role in stopping whatever it was that happened so it wouldn't happen to other people."

"Like a woman who was raped," I said, "but didn't want to testify because of what people might think."

"Exactly."

When we got back to Happy Trails, the first thing I did was look for Rebecca. She was sitting on the patio with a cup of tea reading a book. I sat down with her. "Have you been able to see Dr. Bascom yet?" I asked.

"Saw him first thing this morning," she said. "He had the lab run the tests right away and got back to me just a while ago. He says my blood work is normal."

"That's good. That's a relief."

"Does that mean I'll be all right?"

"I certainly hope so."

"Me, too. I haven't slept in a couple of nights. I hope I can relax now."

"I'm sure you'll be fine."

"Have you found out anything yet?"

"Yes. The pills are made from a compound of both natural and synthetic elements. Much of what's in them is useless and harmless. But some of it can be harmful to some people. Probably a small percentage. But if you happen to be one of those people, the pills can be dangerous."

"So if Walter and Lucile and Georgette were taking the pills, they were part of that small group who reacted badly to the stuff in the pills."

"That's what I suspect."

"But since my blood work came back normal, I'm not in that small group."

"Hopefully."

"But you're not sure."

"There's no way to be sure. But before Georgette died, her doctor commented that her blood work was abnormal in a couple of areas. So that makes me think that some sort of chemical interaction occurred to throw things out of whack."

"That makes sense, I guess," Rebecca said.

"In order to get the pills tested," I said, "We had to go to the police. I had to tell them the story. I didn't use your name. I just said someone at Happy Trails. The guy used to be Harry's partner, so he did us a favor, and one of the techs at the lab did the testing. But a detective now knows that several deaths might be linked to this scam. He wants to look into it. Will you talk to him?"

"I don't want to," Rebecca said, "but I think I should. People have died. And if what's in those pills caused it, I have to do what I can to stop it."

"I'm glad you feel that way. The officer's name is Will Grayson. I'll let him know, and he'll be contacting you."

When I left Rebecca, I went straight to Cybil's office. "I need to meet with you and Linda," I said.

"Sounds important," Cybil said.

"It is."

"Want to give me a hint?"

"I'd rather wait and explain it to both of you."

"Okay. I have time at four forty-five."

"That'll work. You'll let Linda know?"

"I will."

On my way up to our apartment, I ran into Galen Thompson, our oldest resident. Galen is ninety-seven, is almost six feet tall, stands straight, still has a head of thick gray hair, walks a mile everyday and still has his own teeth. "Hi, Harriet," he said.

"Hi, Galen. Got a date for the movie tonight?"

"I do. I'm sharing some popcorn with Ilene. She can't hear worth beans. But I figure that way I don't have to be so careful about what I say."

"Every dark cloud has a silver lining," I said, as I headed for the stairs. "Enjoy the movie."

Harry had the TV on and was reading. "Rebecca says she'll talk to Will," I said as I sat down.

"You have to convince her?"

"No. She knew it was the right thing to do."

"Good. Always better not to have to talk people into something."

"I have a question."

"Okay."

"I assume that whoever is providing these pills to people is guilty of something, but I don't know what. People have died. I don't know that I'd call it murder because they probably didn't think anyone was going to die. So what would you call it?"

"My guess would be negligent homicide," Harry said. "Especially if the person responsible is a doctor or someone who knew or should have known the risks involved and didn't warn the victims."

"Like in the commercials that advertise medications and tell you all the possible side effects."

"Just like that. What they are telling you in effect is that you are taking the medicine at your own risk."

"There wasn't any warning on the *Forever Young* label about possible side effects."

"None that I saw."

"Negligent homicide," I said, more to myself than to Harry.

Chapter 46

It was only twenty after four, so I decided to go talk to Oscar before my meeting with Cybil and Linda. He didn't look good when he answered the door. I can't imagine how I would look if it were only a few days after Harry's death. The very thought was horrid to me. I pushed it out of my head.

"Hi, Harriet," he said. "Come on in. I'd offer you coffee. But I haven't made any."

"It's fine, Oscar, I don't need any coffee."

He sat down in his chair; I sat on the sofa that sat at an angle to his chair. "How you doing?" I asked.

"Okay, I guess, considering the circumstances. We always knew one of us would go first. We talked about it. But I think we both figured it'd be me. I ... I don't know. I mean, physically I'm okay. I eat some; I sleep some. People stop by to check on me. I know I'll be okay. But right now ..." He shrugged. "Lots of men here have lost their wives. I just wasn't prepared for this ... And the way it happened. Everyone thought she was going to be all right."

"I know," I said. "I'm sorry. Would you like me to make some coffee?"

"Coffee would be nice."

I went to the small kitchenette counter—the apartment was exactly like ours—and got the coffee machine going and sat out two mugs. "It'll be ready in a minute," I said when I sat back down. "I need to ask you something."

"Sure."

"Was Georgette taking any new medication?"

"I don't know." He thought about it. Shaking his head, he said, "She didn't mention it. All of her medication is in the bathroom. You can go look if you want."

"You're sure?"

"You think she might have been taking something that caused the brain tumor. If you're right, I'd like to know."

I nodded and went into the bathroom. There was nothing on the vanity. I opened the medicine cabinet. The third bottle from the left looked just like the bottle Rebecca had given me, but the label was turned away. I picked it up. It was the same stuff: Forever Young. I took it with me and went back out to the kitchen counter. The coffee was ready, so I poured two cups and took them across the room, putting them on the coffee table.

Oscar saw that I had a small medicine bottle in my hand. "You find something?"

"Yes. Rebecca Adams got some of this same stuff. It's called Forever Young." I showed him the bottle. We had the stuff analyzed and got the report back just this afternoon. This could have caused the brain tumor."

"Could have," Oscar said.

"There's no way to be certain. But in some people the stuff in these pills can cause heart attacks and brain tumors."

"So Walter and Lucile might have been taking it as well?"

"Perhaps. We don't know yet. I'm going to keep looking. But this may have been what made Georgette sick."

He took the bottle from me, looked at it, shook his head, and handed it back to me.

"Do you know where Georgette got this?"

"No. She took care of all our medications. Where did Rebecca get hers?"

"It came in the mail."

"She still taking it?"

"No."

"Good."

He took a sip of his coffee. Tears filled his eyes. "Find out who's responsible for this, Harriet. Find out and stop them so no one else dies."

Linda and Cybil were waiting for me at four forty-five. "So," I said after sitting down at the small round conference table against the far wall in Cybil's office. "I know you are aware that I've been asking whether or not Walter, Lucile, and Georgette were taking any new medication."

"Yes. Have you made any progress?"

"I have. Because people were talking about the questions I was asking, Rebecca came to me. A couple of months ago she began taking this stuff." I held up the bottle. "It's called Forever Young. It came with a letter that promised all kinds of amazing benefits and asked her not to tell anyone she was taking it. So she didn't. You know how

203

some of us older folks can be sticklers for following directions. But when she heard about my theory, she began to worry. So she came to me and showed me the pills. Harry had one of his cop friends test them."

Linda and Cybil were sitting very still, listening intently.

"The lab report that came back says that most of what's in these is either harmless or useless. But some of what's in here, in some people, can cause severe side effects, including heart attack and brain tumors."

"And Rebecca was taking this?" Linda asked.

"Yes. And so was Georgette."

"What about Walter and Lucile?" Cybil asked.

"I don't know yet."

Cybil's eyes wandered over the walls of her office while she thought.

"Has Rebecca suffered any side effects?" Linda asked.

"No. She had her blood work done, and it came back normal. But before Georgette died, her doctor mentioned that her blood work was abnormal in a couple of areas."

"So you think whatever is in the pills caused Georgette's brain tumor," Linda said.

"I do," I said. "And if Lucile was taking these, it may have caused hers as well. And Walter's heart attack."

"But at the present," Cybil said, "you have no knowledge that either of them were taking it."

"Not yet."

"So you're going to keep pursuing this."

"Yes."

"You said the police lab did the testing," Cybil said. "Does that mean the police are going to be involved?"

"I suspect it does. Rebecca has agreed to talk to them."

Cybil seemed upset. "The negative publicity is not going to be good for business," she said. She took a deep breath and let it out. "But since people have died …"

"There's still lots we don't know," I said. "But we'll get it figured out."

"I hope so," Cybil said.

Chapter 47

Harry was ready to go to dinner when I got back to our apartment. On the way down to the cafeteria, he said, "So how'd Cybil and Linda take it?"

Before I could answer, Ethel came out of her room. "Ethel," I said. She squinted at me. "Ethel, where are your glasses?"

Ethel put her hands to her face. "Dang it. Forgot my glasses."

She turned to go back into her room, and I said, "While you're in there, you might want to check to be sure you haven't forgotten anything else."

She looked somewhat at a loss, so I moved my hands up and down in front of my chest and said, "An article of clothing, perhaps."

She grabbed her substantial breasts, realized what she had done, and said, "Dang. I'm gonna have to make myself a checklist. I'd forget my head if it wasn't screwed on."

She disappeared into her room, and Harry said, "Never a dull moment, is there?"

We started down the stairs, and I said, "So you asked me how Linda and Cybil reacted to the news."

"Yes."

I told him.

"Well, I can understand Cybil's concern from a business point of view. A bunch of people die in her retirement community, even if it's not her fault, and the potential customer list tends to get shorter and shorter."

"I guess," I said. "It's the same way in the hospital. They don't like anyone to know how many patients actually die there. Tends to erode confidence."

Dinner was pulled pork sandwiches with cole slaw and green beans. We filled our plates and sat down at a table for eight. Ed and Jimmy joined us, and in a moment so did Ted and Marilyn. Just as we were digging into our sandwiches, Harry saw Oscar in line. "Hey, listen," he said quietly to everyone at the table, "if Oscar sits with us, don't ask him how he's doing or say how sorry you are or anything like that. He doesn't need to be reminded about what's happened. He needs to get past it, and he can't if everybody keeps bringing it up."

"What'd he say?" Ted asked Marilyn.

Marilyn tried to say quietly what Harry had said, but Ted still didn't get it. So she texted it to him and told him to check his phone. He did and said, "Oh, okay."

Jimmy said, "Getting to be that time, Harry. When we going fishing?"

"I was thinking maybe next Saturday."

"I think next Saturday will work," Ed said, "but I'll have to check with my social secretary. Hey, Jimmy, we got anything scheduled for next Saturday?"

"Actually we do," Jimmy said. "We're going fishing with Harry."

Oscar joined us at the table.

"Let me guess," I said to Ed, "You two are working up a new Abbot and Costello comedy routine for the spring talent show."

"What'd I miss?" Oscar said.

"We're going fishing next Saturday," Ed said.

Oscar looked at Harry. "There room on the boat for me?"

"Absolutely. How about, you Ted? You want to go fishing?"

"I stopped wishing for stuff a long time ago. Doesn't do no good."

"Not wishing," Marilyn said, loud and impatiently. "Fishing. Fishing. On Harry's boat." She made a motion like casting and reeling your line in. "Catching fish."

"Oh. Sure. I love to fish."

"Uh-huh." She leaned in my direction. "The old goat can't hear thunder, but let someone fart and he hears that just fine."

"I didn't fart," Ted said.

"I didn't say you ... Oh just eat your pork."

"I don't need a fork. It's a sandwich."

Harry mumbled something that I suspect was, *never a dull moment.*

The conversation continued on through dessert, shifting topics several times. As we got up from the table, Harry said, "So what are our plans for the evening?"

"Well, there's a nice movie playing tonight in the theater. I thought we might go."

"I'm up for a movie. Is it a western?"

"No, it's not a western. It's about the early life experiences of J.R.R. Tolkien and how they influenced his writing."

"Hmm. Well, at least it's not a romance movie."

"What's wrong with romance movies?"

"Nothing. But I don't need to see them. I'm already romantic enough."

"Uh-huh. The movie doesn't start until seven. There are a couple of calls I need to make before we go."

"Okay. I'm gonna go get my book and sit out on the patio and read until you come get me."

We went to our apartment together and Harry got his book and left. I called Walter's daughter-in-law. "Hi, Susan. It's Harriet Ward, at Happy Trails."

"Oh, sure. Hi, Mrs. Ward. How are you?"

"I'm fine. But I have some news for you." I explained to her about one of our residents coming to me with a bottle of pills she received in the mail—Forever Young. I explained about the lab test on the pills and the potential side effects.

"So what you're saying is that if Walter got some of that stuff in the mail and he was taking it, that might have been what caused his heart attack?"

"Yes. So I was wondering if you still had Walter's things?"

"Yes. I haven't had the heart yet to go through them and get rid of stuff."

"Would you mind looking through his medications and seeing if there is a bottle of Forever Young?"

"Not at all. Hold on. I'll go look right now."

It took a couple of minutes, but when she spoke again, her words gave me a shiver. "I found it. A small brown bottle like a prescription comes in. It says Forever Young."

"Are there still pills in it?"

"Yes. Ten or fifteen, I'd guess."

"Would you be able to send it to me? It's a long drive from Odessa. "

"Sure. I can mail it to you."

"That's great," I said. "And would you put the bottle in a sandwich bag and label and sign it?"

"To make it official evidence?"

"Yes."

"I'll put it in the mail first thing in the morning. You should get it day after tomorrow. What's your address?"

I gave it to her, and she thanked me. Then, before she disconnected and almost as an after thought she added, "I can't believe that someone would give old people medication that would kill them."

"Me, either. We'll find who did it."

Since I'd hit the jackpot with Walter's family, I figured I'd call Lucile's as well. After her husband had died, she'd given me her niece's contact information … *just in case something happens to me.* Her niece, Patricia, was in her mid-thirties, and other than the unfriendly sister-in-law, was the only family Lucile had left.

I called her.

"Yeah, I have all of it," Patricia said. "I haven't had the time yet to go through it."

I explained what I was curious about and why.

"So she was taking something that caused her brain tumor?"

"She might have been."

"And this stuff is called what?"

"Forever Young."

"Hold on. I'll go check."

It took her longer than it had taken Susan, but when she came back she said, "Yeah, she was taking it. There a bottle that's about half full."

"Can you send it to me. The police will need to see it."

"Sure."

I gave her our mailing address and asked her to put it in a baggie and label and sign it. She said she would.

"I'll mail it first thing in the morning."

I found Harry on the patio where he said he would be. I sat down with him and explained what I'd found.

"Impressive," he said. "You'd have made a good detective."

"It's kind of satisfying when the pieces begin falling into place, isn't it?"

Harry smiled. "What's your next step?"

"I guess we need to figure out who mailed the stuff to them."

"Check the postmark on the box or whatever packaging it came in."

"I hadn't thought of that. I wonder if Rebecca still has one of the packages the stuff came in."

It was nearly seven. Time for the movie. Harry and I went to the theater, got some popcorn, and found some seats on the end of the row. Harry always wants to sit on the end of a row. He didn't especially care if we were near the front or the back, as long as he was on the end of the row. I guess it's an old man thing. When he has to get up to go to the

211

restroom, and he *will* have to get up to go to the restroom, he doesn't want to have to climb over people.

Rebecca came in a few minutes after we sat down. "I'll be right back," I said to Harry. I went up to where Rebecca was and sat in the empty seat beside her. "Do you have the box or package the pills came in?" I asked.

"No. I didn't keep it."

"When do you think you'll get another bottle?"

"Should be any day now, I think."

"Will you save the packaging for me?"

"Of course. Why?"

"We need to check the postmark."

Chapter 48

The next few days were hectic. The assistant director, Esther Meer, was busy trying to get residents to agree to participate in the spring talent show—an event that was always more show than talent. The Happy Trails fifteen-passenger bus was rear-ended on the way back from the mall. No one was injured, but to hear them talk, you'd think they'd survived the apocalypse. One of the toilets in one of the lady's ground floor restrooms backed up and overflowed. The smell was delightful. Fortunately, the plumbers got the problem resolved, and a cleaning company got the mess that had spilled out into the hallway cleaned up in a few hours. Then it rained, and it became apparent that the recent hail storm had damaged the roof, and several of the third-floor residents had leaks.

Then, as if those things weren't enough, Alice Garvey, our cook, came down with the flu, and Cybil brought in a temp to cook for us, who, apparently, had her own ideas about senior nutrition. The woman was from Boston. She and her husband had just recently moved to

Abilene when her husband had accepted a teaching position at Abilene Christian University. She was a nice young lady who looked to be in her late thirties. Her name was Kathleen, and she had no idea how to feed a bunch of meat-loving old Texans.

As we went through the buffet line for Tuesday dinner, there was no brisket, no pulled pork, no fried catfish or crappie. No ham steaks. There were a lot of vegetables, some sort of chicken casserole, sliced turkey, sliced cheese, and some small seven-grain rolls for making small sandwiches with the turkey and cheese. It was probably very healthy and probably met some published guidelines for the nutritional needs of senior citizens. But it was not the kind of food we were used to. After dinner, I noticed several people talking to Cybil. I was pretty sure they were complaining, and I was pretty sure I knew how the conversation would go—*we pay a lot of money to live here, and the least you can do is get a cook who will feed us real food.*

Breakfast the next morning was our standard fare: scrambled eggs, sausage, hash browns, English muffins, oatmeal, yogurt, and fresh fruit. The mutiny was quelled … at least until lunchtime.

A little before nine, it was discovered that the pool heater had gone out sometime during the night. Harry was not happy about having to workout in the gym instead of going for his morning swim. Cybil got the maintenance man, Joe, working on the heater problem. By lunchtime, several people had gone to see Linda complaining about flu symptoms. When it rains it pours.

While all this was going on, I decided to call Kendra Williams in Sweetwater and Judy Pearson in Cisco to bring them up to speed on the investigation.

"So the three people who passed away at Happy Trails," Kendra said, "were taking this Forever Young stuff."

"Yes."

"And according to the lab report, it contains stuff that can cause heart attacks and brain tumors?"

"Yes."

"Why would the FDA approve a drug like that?"

"It's not FDA approved," I said.

"And you're wondering if my mother was taking it."

"Yeah. Do you still have any of her medications?"

"I do," she said. "Hold on."

"Yeah," Kendra said, after a few moments. "There was a bottle of it in with her other medications."

"Was there a box or mailing envelope that it came in?"

"Didn't see one."

I asked if she could put it in a baggy, label it, and bring it to me. She said she would.

Judy Pearson's mother was taking it, too. There was no mailing package. She agreed to bring the bottle to me.

Chapter 49

It was Wednesday morning. It had been four days since Rebecca had said her next delivery of Forever Young should be coming soon. Maybe it would arrive in the mail today. Kendra and Judy had dropped off their mothers' bottles of Forever Young, and the bottles Susan and Patricia sent had arrived in the mail.

Joe had gotten the pool heater fixed, and Harry was swimming. I was sitting on the patio with a cup of coffee, thinking about what to do next when I saw Rebecca and Will come out onto the patio. Rebecca pointed to me, Will said something to her, she went back inside, and Will came and sat down across from me.

I said, "You've interviewed Rebecca, I take it."

"I did."

"Was what she told you helpful?"

"Same basic information you gave me, but she said she'd testify if it became necessary."

"Good. I've got some new information I think you will find useful."

"Tell me."

"As it turns out. The other of our residents who passed away, Walter and Lucile, were also talking Forever Young. I have the bottles of the stuff that was in with their other medications."

"That's good work," Will said.

"And," I said, "so was a lady who passed away in Cisco and another in Sweetwater."

"And both of them lived in retirement communities?"

"Yes."

"You have their names?"

"I have more than that. I also have their bottles of the stuff."

"How'd you manage that?"

"We found their daughters, talked to them, explained what had happened here, and asked them to check their mothers' medications."

"And the stuff was there."

"Yep. And they brought it to me. In a baggie signed and sealed."

"Maybe we should hire you instead of David."

"Very funny. I have all the stuff up in our apartment. Want me to bring it down to you?"

"If it's not too much trouble."

"No trouble at all."

Just as I was getting up, Harry, showered and dressed after his swim, came out onto the patio. "Figures," Harry said. "Leave Will alone for two minutes and he always manages to find the prettiest girl in the place and sits down to talk with her."

"Uh-huh," I said, unable to keep from smiling. "Buy him a cup of coffee while I go get the stuff I've collected."

As few minutes later, I gave everything I had collected to Will, and Harry and I walked him out to the front entrance. He thanked me, and said he would follow up on it. As Harry and I were meandering back through the facility, Harry said, "What's bothering you?"

"I'm worried that there might be other people who are still taking the drug."

"There might be."

"They need to be warned."

"What do you think is the best way to do that?" Harry asked.

"I don't know. I guess we could make an announcement at lunch or dinner. Tell everyone how dangerous it is."

"You could."

"Or I could talk to everyone individually."

"That's an option, too. Which one do you think is best?"

"Well, it's a lot more work, but to make sure everyone really understands, I think I should talk to everyone individually, and they should be given a copy of the lab report so they can see for themselves how dangerous it is."

"Sounds like a plan," Harry said.

"I'll start after lunch. What are you going to be doing?"

"Playing golf."

I took my copy of the lab report to Linda, explained what I was going to do, and asked her to make fifty copies for me. I figured one copy was enough for a couple. At one o'clock, I began talking to people. I explained to them that Walter, Lucile, and Georgette, and two people who lived in other retirement communities who had also passed away, were taking Forever Young. I explained how dangerous it was and gave them a copy of the lab report. By four thirty, I had talked to just about everybody. Thirty-six people had gotten an initial bottle of Forever Young. Several of them had simply tossed it. But five men and eight women had been taking it. They said they'd stop immediately. I asked them to put the bottle in a baggie and bring it to me so I could pass it on to the police. They assured me they would. I also asked if any of them had the packaging the pills came it. One woman, Valerie Lakeside, did. She brought it to me. No postmark.

Harry was in our apartment reading when I went up. "Golf game go well?" I asked.

"It did. I birdied two holes. How'd your afternoon go?"

I told him how it went and then explained about Valerie Lakeside. "But there was no postmark on the box," I said.

"So it didn't come through the mail," Harry said.

"Then how ..." I stopped mid-sentence. "That means someone who has access to our mailboxes put the pills in Valerie's mailbox."

Harry took a deep breath and let it out. "That's a disturbing thought, isn't it?"

"Who would have access to our mailboxes?"

"Good question. Maybe Cybil knows."

Chapter 50

Harry and I were about half way through dinner, enjoying the conversation with the people at our round eight-person table. Ed and Jimmy had given us a sample of their talent show routine. Edna had showed us pictures of her new great-grandson. BettyJo told us about her latest dream—that if any more liberals got elected to the Texas state legislature, all the beaches in the state were going to become nude beaches.

"Until you said that," Jimmy said to BettyJo, "I could never come up with a single reason to vote for a liberal."

That got a laugh from everyone at the table except our resident liberal, Dan Black, who started to say something but realized he was outnumbered and changed his mind.

"I heard you were going to the gun show," Harry said to Sandra.

"Yep," she said. Sandra was widowed last year and came to live at Happy Trails about nine months ago. She's seventy-six, stands just a tad over five foot tall and weighs right at a hundred pounds. "It was a good show. Nice mix of new and used guns, and of rifles and handguns. Got myself a Glock 42. Put a hundred rounds through it at the range this afternoon. Has a nice feel to it. Very little recoil."

This was more than Dan could take so he said, "Why would you feel the need to own a gun? Are you that frightened?"

"I don't just own a gun," Sandra said, "I have a license to carry. And no, I'm not frightened. I'm just determined that I'm going to do everything I can to keep from becoming a victim should a situation ever arise."

"How are you going to become a victim living here? This is a safe place."

"So far it is. But I'm not here all the time. I'm out and about. And there isn't any place that's completely safe all the time. So I carry an insurance policy. Probably won't ever have to use it. But the old saying holds true: better to have it and not need it than to need it and not have it."

"Could you really shoot someone?"

She locked eyes with him and said, "I hope to God I never have to. But to save my life or the life of another person, you bet I could."

Dan just shook his head, apparently unable to cope with the reality of a sweet little old lady packing heat.

Edna and Sandra decided to forego dessert, so when we came back to the table with our evening coffee and pie, two spots had opened up. As we sat down, Gilda sat down beside me. "Here are my pills," she said, handing me a baggie that was labeled and signed. "Glad to get rid of the blasted things," she said. "They're kind of chalky and hard to swallow. And I don't think they did anything anyway. I hope you catch whoever sent them to us."

"Me, too."

Over the course of the evening, while we were playing 42 with Rick and Nancy, nine more people brought me their unused pills. Most of them expressed some level of outrage at being lied to.

By nine thirty, we had finished four rounds of 42. Harry and I won three of them. We said good night to Rick and Nancy and went up to our apartment. At ten, Harry turned on Fox News and we listened to Shannon Bream brief us on the day's events. A few minutes into it, my phone rang. It was Nikki.

"Hi, Grandma. I didn't wake you, did I?"

"Nope. Sitting here watching the news. What's up?"

"It happened."

"It did."

"Yes."

"Are you going to tell me what *it* is, or do I have to guess?"

"Dad brought a girl home. Well, a woman."

"When you say *brought a woman home*, what do you mean?"

"A date. Well, actually before he brought her home, he took us out to eat. We went to dinner."

"I see."

Harry was now looking at me, listening to one side of the conversation. To help him out, I put the call on speaker, and he muted the TV.

"And then after dinner," Nikki said, "we came home and watched a movie—one of the newer Jack Ryan movies."

"And?"

"And what?"

222

"You know perfectly well what."

"She's okay I guess. Her name's Joyce. She's about Dad's age, I think. She doesn't look old yet."

"How nice for her."

"I guess. Anyway, I thought you should know. Since Dad applied for the cop job, he's been like a different person. Happy and positive and all. It's been nice."

"I'm glad to hear it. Has he been seeing Joyce long?"

"I don't know. I didn't want to ask too many questions."

"Well, if your father asked her out, I'm sure she's a very nice lady."

"I don't know. Maybe. You used to think Mom was nice. Look how that ended up."

She had me there. "Sometimes people change. But when your parents were first married, she was a nice person. And I'm sure in many ways she still is."

"Not in any of the ways that count."

She was upset. I wondered if she knew why. "What are you upset about, Nikki?"

There was a long silence. I waited. Harry was watching the TV screen, but I knew he was listening and waiting, too.

"I don't want Dad to get hurt again."

There it was. The girl was becoming a young woman. She was beginning to understand. I was proud of her.

"Nikki," I said, "if you don't open yourself up to the possibility of pain, you deny yourself the possibility of love."

More silence. She was thinking.

Finally, she said, "Jeez, Grandma. You're like the love philosopher. How do you know all this stuff?"

"I'm old."

Chapter 51

The next morning, I explained to Cybil about the lack of a postmark on the package Valerie's bottle of Forever Young came in.

"Really," Cybil said.

"Is it possible that someone here put the package in her box?"

Cybil bristled. "Well, I certainly hope not."

"Other than the residents who have a key to their box," I asked, "who else would have a key and be able to open the boxes?"

"Well, the postman has a master key that will open all the boxes. And I have a master key. If someone loses their key or leaves without returning it, we have to be able to open the box."

"Of course. Is your master key in a secure location so that no one could borrow it?"

"I keep the key in a locked box in a locked cabinet," Cybil said. She picked up her keys that were lying on her desk, selected a small silver key and swiveled her chair around to the credenza behind her desk. She unlocked a cabinet door, removed a small metal box and set it on her desk. Then, using another key, she unlocked a drawer in her desk and withdrew a set of keys. Selecting a key, she opened the box. She turned the box so I could see. It was filled with keys.

"These are the master keys to every door in the place. One master key opens all the apartment doors, another all the office doors, another the storage doors, and so forth."

She looked in the box, moved her index finger back and forth over the keys, moved some of the keys around, and finally said, "Oh, my. The master key to the mailboxes is missing. How could that be? Other than you, who I just showed, no one knew where the key was or how to get to it. How could it be missing?"

"When was the last time you used it?"

She thought. "It would have been months ago. I don't have reason to use it very often."

"So you have no idea how long it's been missing."

"No."

I went out to the pool area where Harry was still swimming. I didn't want to interrupt his workout, so I brought a cup of coffee and sat down in a chair to watch him. He was an excellent swimmer, moving easily through the water. All the time he spent in the pool kept his body slim, firm, and muscular. He was a good-looking old man. Maybe I should spend more time in the pool.

When Harry finished his swim and dried off, he sat down beside me. I explained to him about my conversation with Cybil.

"So somebody other than Cybil has access to the mailboxes."

"Yes."

"So all you have to do," Harry said, "is find out who."

"Where would I even begin to do something like that?"

"I'd start by finding out who has access to Cybil's office."

"I don't know if they do," I said, "but Linda and Esther might have access. The cleaning people do. They clean her office each night. I can't imagine Linda or Esther stealing the mailbox key so they could hand out free samples of a dangerous drug."

"Maybe whoever it was didn't know it was dangerous," Harry said.

"Linda's a nurse. She knows what the possibilities are."

"What about Esther?"

"Esther doesn't have the training Linda does, but common sense should …"

"If common sense were in play," Harry said, "No one would have taken the stuff."

"Never underestimate public stupidity?" I said.

"Something like that. Especially when it comes with the promise of being young forever."

"Still," I said, "I can't see Linda or Esther involved in something as horrible as this."

"I understand," Harry said. "But if whoever it was didn't have access to the lab report, maybe they didn't understand the potential for danger."

"You're saying I shouldn't rule out anyone."

227

"Ruling out anyone in advance is a luxury a good investigator can't afford."

I thought for a moment. "What if someone approached one of the cleaning people? Offered them money to get the mailbox key?"

"Okay, suppose that happened and someone got hold of the mailbox key. When would they have access to the mailboxes without someone noticing? The place is locked up at night. Can't get in without the fob to open the system. In the day, someone would notice a strange person messing with the mailboxes."

"Then how'd the stuff get in there?" I asked, feeling and sounding frustrated.

"I don't know."

We went up to our apartment so Harry could shower and dress. He sat and read for a while; I worked a puzzle. Just before lunch, Will called Harry to give him an update. Harry put the call on speaker.

"First thing I did when I got back yesterday is look for who owns the P.O. box the reply card and the survey goes back to."

"And?" I said.

"It's owned by a dummy corporation. Which is owned by another dummy corporation, and so on."

"So that's a dead end," Harry said.

"As dead as they get."

I explained that we had one of the boxes the Forever Young came in, but that it lacked a postmark.

"So someone other than the United States Postal Service put it in the mailboxes."

I told him about the stolen master key.

"Okay," Will said. "I'll have to come in there and talk to the people who have access to her office."

"There are also the two other retirement communities," I said.

"Cisco and Sweetwater," Will said.

"Yeah."

"You got any thoughts, Harry?"

"Harriet mentioned the cleaning people. They have access to Cybil's office. Might be interesting to see if the same cleaning company cleans the other retirement facilities."

"Okay, I'll put that on my to-do list. If you come up with anything else, give me a call."

Chapter 52

On the way to the cafeteria for dinner, we saw Bill and Wanda Gospic, friends from church, coming through the front entrance. I assumed they were coming to see Carrie Lawry, a Happy Trails resident who is a member of our church and who hasn't been feeling well. Harry and I had just come from Carrie's apartment, having stopped in to see how she was doing. Her pacemaker wasn't getting the job done any longer, and she needed an upgrade, and one of her medications was making her dizzy. No wonder she hadn't been feeling well. Harry and I took a detour from the cafeteria to say hello to Bill and Wanda and gave them an update on Carrie. After visiting with us briefly, they went on up to see Carrie.

As we headed back toward the cafeteria, I happened to look out through the large glass windows across the front of the building. In the parking lot, approaching the building, I was the young woman I'd seen a few days before. I had assumed her to be someone researching retirement communities for her parents. But as I watched her, I couldn't shake the feeling that I'd seen her in some other context. As she came in the front door, I elbowed Harry. "See that young woman?"

"Uh-huh."

"She looks very familiar to me."

"We saw her on the evening news several days ago. She's the vice president of a Dallas-based pharmaceutical company ... Pharm ... Pharm ... Pharmakon."

"You and your memory," I said. "You're as old as Moses and you have the memory of a thirty year old."

"That's not all I've got that resembles a man of thirty."

"Yeah, but your feet don't count."

"My feet?"

"You have young feet."

"I wasn't talking about my feet."

"I know. I wonder what she's doing here."

He mumbled something else and then said, "She's probably just shopping for a place for her parents. Young people come here all the time doing that."

"I suppose. You're sure she's the woman we saw on TV?"

"Pretty sure."

As she got to the front door, I looked back down the other way toward Cybil's office. Cybil was standing at her door. She smiled and waved at me.

Harry and I went on to the cafeteria and got in line. The fill-in cook was still struggling with what to feed us. The main course choices were chicken breast on a bed of rice with a medley of vegetables, or tuna casserole and a medley of vegetables. There were also some dry, room temperature rolls. Alice always heated the rolls and glazed them with melted butter. Cybil was going to hear about this.

Harry and I selected the chicken and passed on the cold, dry bread. We sat down at a table with Elizabeth and Marty. Marty Winston was a retired newspaper editor who now wrote a weekly Op Ed for the Abilene newspaper.

"So what's your article for this week, Marty?" Harry asked.

"The Problem With Term Limits," Marty said.

"You realize your swimming upstream, right?"

"Aw, those dummies aren't thinking it through." Marty said. "World politics today is too complicated for a bunch of amateurs. I can just see it now. A middle school science teacher, an insurance agent, an actress, and a clown who graduated from some third rate law school who can't making a living chasing ambulances, getting themselves elected to Congress where they end up sitting on the intelligence committee making decisions about Russia, China, and North Korea. Or on the finance committee, or the judicial committee. The country's got enough problems as it is without sending a bunch of ignorant amateurs to Washington."

Elizabeth smiled. "Marty's passionate about politics," she said.

"He's also right," Harry said.

As we ate, Cybil came by our table with the young woman I'd seen. "Harriet," she said, "I'd like you to meet, Denise Griffin. Denise, Harriet Ward."

I stood and shook hands with Denise. She seemed a little stiff, I thought.

"Denise is a vice president at Pharakon, a pharmaceutical company in Dallas. I called her to see if she knew anything about this Forever Young stuff that some of our people have been taking."

"Really," I said.

"Yes," Denise said. "She told me about the deaths. It's just awful."

"So, have you heard about Forever Young?"

"I have not. But I'm going to ask some of my people to look into it. See if they can come up with anything."

"That would be great. We can use all the help we can get."

"Well," Cybil said, "we'll let you get back to your dinner. I just wanted to introduce you."

As they started to leave, Denise said, "Oh, one other thing. Our company does a quarterly newsletter that goes out to a bunch of senior communities in the southwest. I'd like to run a brief story about this Forever Young stuff and what you're doing to try to stop it. Could I take your picture to run with the article?" She had her phone out, looking expectantly at me.

"Well," I said, "I'm not really ready for a photograph."

"Nonsense. You look great."

"Well, I guess it's okay."

I stood and smiled and Denise took a photo with her phone.

"Thank you. I think people will be really interested in the article."

Cybil and Denise left and we finished dinner with Marty telling us about other articles he intended to write:

Free Stuff—The Creation of a Dependent Society, Why Borders Exist, What It Means To Be A Society Of Equals, Progressive Taxation—Unequal Treatment Under The Law.

Elizabeth seemed fascinated. I doubted she was over Walter yet, but Marty was single. Maybe to two of them would become friends. You never know.

Chapter 53

The next morning, the new cook, frustrated with having to satisfy the tastes of the Happy Trails residents, quit. Good. Cybil turned the kitchen over to Gloria, Alice's assistant, which is what most of us thought she should have done in the first place. Rumor had it, however, that Alice was better and would be coming back tomorrow. Gloria wouldn't enjoy her victory long this time around, but the next time Alice was away, Gloria would be a shoo-in for the job. The other residents who had been sick began feeling better and returned to the land of the living. Things seemed to be getting back to normal at Happy Trails.

After breakfast I felt like working on my Greek urn, so while Harry was swimming, I went to the ceramics room. Several years ago Harry and I took a cruise of the islands of the Aegean that included a couple of days in Athens. We had visited the Acropolis and bought all the usual tourist stuff, including a photo of the Acropolis from a location somewhere across the city. That was the image I wanted to paint on my urn. I selected a very fine point brush and began working very slowly to reproduce the image on my urn. After an hour, it was apparent that it was going to take several hour-long sessions to finish it. That was okay by me. It wasn't like there was a deadline. I put it in my locker along with my paints and brushes and went to find Harry.

I found him in our apartment, showered and dressed, working at the computer. "What are you up to?" I asked. "You're not on that *Sports Illustrated Swimsuit* site again are you?"

"Yep. I was planning on buying you a new swimsuit for your birthday, and I thought I'd look to see what kind would be most flattering to your voluptuous figure."

"Uh-huh."

I walked up behind him. "That's the Pharmakon website."

"Yeah," he said. "Something about Denise Griffin seemed a little off to me, so I thought I'd wander around their website for a while. See if anything jumped out at me."

"See anything yet?"

"I've been looking for that quarterly newsletter she said she wrote. Can't seem to find it."

"Maybe it's not online," I said. "Maybe it's just a printed publication."

"Thirty years ago that might have been the case. But not today. If they had a quarterly publication of some kind, it'd be online."

"So what does that mean?"

"It means she lied," Harry said.

"Why would she lie about writing a newsletter?"

"I don't know. Maybe that's not the only thing she lied about."

We tossed around different possibilities about what Ms. Griffin might have been lying about, but couldn't come up with anything that seemed to make sense, so we decided to go to the mall. Harry said he needed a couple of new mysteries, so we spent some time in the bookstore. He went to the mystery section while I browsed in the history section. I found something I wanted, and found Harry still trying to make up his mind.

"I thought Robert Parker was your favorite," I said.

"He is. But I've read all of his stuff at least twice. I need something different."

"How different?"

"Depends. What'd you have in mind?"

"Have you ever read Agatha Christie?"

"The old British dame?"

"Dame in what sense?"

"What?" he asked, frowning.

"She was awarded the designation of Dame in 1971."

"So she was literally an old Dame," Harry said.

"Ha. She probably wouldn't appreciate you putting it exactly that way, but yes."

"You think I'd like her stuff?"

"You might like her Hercule Poirot stuff. The murders he unraveled were usually quite complex. Only the Bible and Shakespeare have sold more copies than her stuff."

"Really. Haven't we seen some Poirot movies?"

"*Murder on the Orient Express. Death on the Nile.*"

"Yeah. Those were pretty good. Maybe I'll give the old Dame a try."

He bought two Poirot mysteries and then went with me to Penny's. He waited patiently while I tried on two pair of slacks, gray and brown, and two tops, light blue and a soft yellow.

Chapter 54

By twelve thirty, we were back at Happy Trails, and having lunch, sitting at a table for eight with only five of the seats taken. Dan Black was with us, along with Rachel and Bill Ford. Rachel had been an English teacher, Bill an economics professor. Dan was on another of his rants, this time complaining about capitalism.

"It isn't working," he said. "We need to do away with it."

Normally, Harry will push back on whatever liberal dribble Dan is advocating. But this time since Bill was an economist, I knew Harry would be happy to let Bill deal with Dan.

"So what is it," Bill asked, "that you think capitalism is supposed to be doing that it's not doing?"

"What?"

"You say capitalism isn't working. In what way is it not working? What is it supposed to be doing that it's not doing?"

"It's supposed to be raising the income of the working class, reducing the amount of income inequality that we have. It's supposed to be an equalizing feature. But it's not. It's just making the rich richer."

"I don't know where you got that idea," Bill said, "but you couldn't be more wrong. Capitalism is an economic system that allows people to invest or to do business—making and selling something, providing a service, or offering a marketable skill—in an effort to make money. People who are using the system, people who have a desirable skill set are selling those skills to companies and making money. People who have a product to manufacture are making it and marketing it and making money. People who have a service to offer, if it's a desirable service, are marketing it and making money. In some cases people are making a lot of money.

Bill was remaining remarkably calm as he spoke.

"Do you know who's not benefiting from capitalism, Dan? Uneducated people who have no marketable skills, service, or product to offer. And do you know why they have no marketable skills, service, or product? Because they didn't go to school and develop any marketable skills. So what's the problem? Is it that capitalism as an economic system isn't working? Or that people who have nothing to offer aren't able to utilize the system? And if they're not, whose fault is that?"

Dan regrouped and came at it from another angle. I had to give him credit, he wasn't easily deterred.

While Dan and Bill butted heads over capitalism vs. socialism, I noticed that Cybil had come into the cafeteria with a couple who looked to be in their fifties. The man had longish sandy brown hair and wore glasses. The woman had shoulder-length brown hair and also wore glasses. Cybil was gesturing, pointing, and explaining—giving a tour. The couple was too young to be looking for a place for themselves. Probably looking for a place for their parents. I looked at Harry, and he was watching Cybil and the couple. The man took out his phone, tapped on the screen, looked at whatever he had called up and then scanned the room. I could sense Harry tense up just a bit.

From across the room, the man and the woman first looked in our direction and then began walking toward us. Their movements were relaxed but precise. As the man approached, he dropped his phone into the breast pocket of his sport jacket and with his right hand reached behind him. As he did, so did Harry. Harry is getting old, but when he needs to, he can still move quickly. The man and Harry came up with their guns at just about the same time, but Harry was a fraction of a second faster and fired first. The man got off a shot as he fell backward. The shot went high into the wall near the ceiling.

The woman was bringing up her gun, but Harry turned his weapon on her and yelled, "FREEZE!"

She did. Good thing, too. When I was able to pull my eyes from the woman and look around, there were probably a dozen guns pointed at her.

Chapter 55

"Put the gun on the floor," Harry said to the woman, his weapon pointed at her. "Slowly."

She did.

"Now," he ordered, "hands behind your head."

She did as she was told.

"Now lay down on the floor, facedown."

Keeping his gun on her, Harry crossed the room to her and picked up her weapon. Then, keeping his eyes on her, he picked up the man's weapon.

"Someone get me something to tie her hands with."

In a moment, one of the girls from the kitchen handed him some twine. He holstered his weapon, and Harry tied her hands behind her. Only then did he take out his phone and call Will.

When you've shot and killed someone, even if you're a retired police officer with seventy witnesses, it's good to have a cop present who can vouch for you.

"Hope you're not busy," Harry said. "I just shot and killed an assassin. We have his partner in custody … About seventy of them … Okay."

Harry put his phone away, and said, "Okay everybody, listen up. Put your weapons away and sit down. Stay where you are. When the police arrive, answer their questions honestly. Don't volunteer information. If they ask you if you are armed, tell them and show them your license to carry. Otherwise, just wait patiently."

Harry put the two guns on the table and then knelt beside the dead man on the floor. He studied him for a moment and then reached over and pulled a wig off the man. He had short dark hair that was beginning to gray. Harry removed his glasses and pulled the mustache from under his nose. The man was quite ordinary looking.

Harry stood, put the items of the simple disguise on the table next to the guns, and knelt beside the woman who was still face down on the floor. He rolled her over, studied her, and removed the wig and glasses she was wearing. Her real hair was short and blond. She was younger than the disguise made her look.

Harry put them on the table with the other items and sat down.

"How'd you know he was going for a gun?" I asked.

"The look in his eyes. His body language. After forty years you can read the signs."

The police arrived in a few minutes with the EMT's right behind them. Will got there a few minutes later and took charge of the scene. He had an officer cuff the woman with real handcuffs and put her in a squad car. While the

EMT's examined the man, Will asked Harry what happened. He took notes as Harry explained.

"That the way you saw it?" he asked me when Harry finished.

"Exactly," I said.

Will nodded and wrote in his notebook. Then he questioned Cybil, who was pretty shaken.

"They came asking for a tour," Cybil said. "Said they needed to find a place for her mother. So I gave them the standard tour. When I brought them in here to show them the cafeteria, they walked straight to Harry's table and pulled their guns. Good thing Harry was faster."

Will had several uniformed officers begin taking statements from other residents, letting them leave the cafeteria once they had explained what happened. The crime scene guys showed up and photographed the body.

As the dining room began to clear out, I looked around for Cybil. She was sitting at a small table by herself, looking stunned. I sat down opposite her. "You okay?" I asked.

"They were going to kill you," she said.

"That appeared to be their intent."

"Why? Why would they want to kill you?"

"I don't know. Maybe the woman will explain."

Chapter 56

The next morning, Friday morning, after Harry had gone for his swim and I for my walk, Will found us in the cafeteria having our mid-morning cup of coffee.

"When we offered her a deal," Will said, "she became a real chatter-box."

"Amazing how that works," Harry said. "So what did you learn?"

"She and her partner were hired assassins. A third party hired them to kill Harriet and Cybil. There was a photo of each of them on their phones."

Will took out his phone and showed us the photo of me.

"That's the photo that Denise Griffin took the other day," I said. "Why would that picture be on the phone of two hired assassins?" And then it hit me. "It was Denise Griffin who hired them," I said, as much to myself as to Harry and Will.

"It's at least a possibility," Will said.

"She's probably the one behind the Forever Young scam," Harry said. "And you uncovered it."

It was all coming at me too fast. I ran it all through my head. "So her motive was revenge? She wanted to kill me because I exposed the whole thing?"

"Probably," Harry said.

"But why would she want to kill Cybil, too. Cybil didn't ..."

"Or did she?" Will asked.

"Maybe we should go ask her," Harry said.

The three of us went to Cybil's office. The door was closed and locked. I asked the receptionist, Chloe, if she knew where Cybil was.

"She hasn't been in yet this morning."

Will showed her his badge. "I need to get into her office. Who has a key?"

Chloe thought for a moment. "Esther, the assistant director has a key, but she's not in yet."

"Call her, please."

Chloe called Esther and handed the phone to Will. He explained who he was and what he needed. He listened, thanked her, and handed the receiver back to Chloe.

"She was already on her way," Will said. "She'll be here in a few minutes."

I was having trouble getting a handle on what was happening. It was beginning to look like Cybil was somehow involved, and Denise wanted her out of the way. The whole thing was beginning to feel like a TV mystery movie.

Esther arrived, and Will showed her his badge. She retrieved a master key from her office and opened Cybil's office door. It only took a moment before it was apparent

246

that Cybil's office had been cleaned out. Drawers had been emptied; files were missing. I called her cell. It rang several times and then rolled over to voice mail.

"She's not answering her phone," I said. "Something's wrong."

"Do you know where she lives?" Will asked.

"On Elmwood. On the north side of 14th."

"I'll check it out."

"Can we ride along?" I asked.

"Sure."

It took about five minutes to get there. Will pulled into the circular drive, stopping behind Cybil's burgundy Escalade. The Escalade's hatch was open, and was partially filled with suitcases and boxes. As we were getting out of Will's car, Cybil came out of her front door carrying another box. For a split second it looked as if she were going to run, but then resolve replaced the fear and she said, "I know this must look suspicious, but this is all just so horrendous— friends dying, assassins trying to kill people. I can't stand it. I need to get away for a while."

Cybil's eyes were locked onto mine. Will must have sensed that I was figuring it out, and he remained quiet. I considered Cybil for a long moment and then said, "It was you who put the pills in the mailboxes, wasn't it?"

"I don't know what you're talking about," she said. "I didn't put anything anywhere."

"Yes, you did. The question is, why?"

Will took out his phone and called someone, while Cybil stood defiantly, still holding the box she had when she'd come out of the house.

"Jim," Will said, "we need to pick up Denise Griffin in Dallas, at Pharmakon … Yeah, she one of the VPs … Conspiracy to commit murder … Okay, thanks."

"When they start questioning her," I said, "it will all come out."

"She's right," Will said. "If you cooperate, it will go easier for you. Remember, she tried to have you killed."

After a brief pause and a deep breath, Cybil put the box on the ground and said, "Do you have any idea what it costs to run a place like Happy Trails?"

Chapter 57

Monday morning, while most of us were just finishing up breakfast, an assistant DA showed up with the police and Cybil. Standing in the entry to the cafeteria, Cybil said, "The district attorney was kind enough to let me come and talk to you. I've done terrible things, and I am deeply sorry. I didn't know anyone would die. I'm so sorry. I haven't been charged yet, so I don't know what's going to happen to me, but I wanted to explain what's going on. I'm going to sell Happy Trails. Until there's a buyer, a court appointed trustee will be managing the facility. They assure me that on a day-to-day basis, nothing will change for you."

Overcome with grief, she needed a moment to compose herself, then she said, "Here's why all this happened. Running a place like this is very expensive. The insurance premiums alone are astronomical. I couldn't bring myself to raise prices and ask people for more money. So when Denise Griffin contacted me offering me a way to make a considerable amount of money, I agreed. I swear, I didn't know anyone would get hurt, let alone die. You see,

249

Pharmakon had created a new drug they called Forever Young. Mostly it was just vitamins, but it had some other stuff in it that was supposed to be the next age-reversing miracle drug. But it wasn't FDA approved. The process takes so long … well, Denise, who was in charge of the drug's development, wanted to test it independently of the FDA and then present them with the findings."

She paused again to breathe.

"After I pay the expenses here each year, my income is less than seventeen thousand dollars. I was going under. So when Denise contacted me, along with a number of other retirement community managers or owners, and asked us to help her, I agreed. She was offering a lot of money if we would help her test the drug. I needed the money. I didn't know anyone would get hurt. I'm sorry."

As the police were taking Cybil away, Elizabeth spoke up. "What will happen to her?"

"We don't know yet," the assistant DA said. "There are fifteen other owners or managers of various retirement centers who also helped distribute the drug. We're still trying to figure out what to do with all of them."

The room was eerily quiet for several minutes after Cybil was taken out. Then, little by little, people began talking.

"I wonder," I said, "how anyone smart enough to become a corporate vice president could be stupid enough to do the things Dense Griffin has done, especially hiring killers to kill people. How could she possibly think she'd get away with that?"

"Maybe she didn't get to be vice president because she was smart," Harry said.

"That may be. But still, how could she think those two could just walk in here and kill two people and no one would connect her to it?"

"Actually," Harry said, "she only made one miscalculation. If it hadn't have been for the photo of you on the killer's phone, we wouldn't have connected it to her. The shooters would have walked in here in disguise, shot two people and walked out. They would have driven away, probably in a stolen car. They'd have taken off the disguises, driven to where their car was, ditched the stolen car, and driven away with no one looking for them. It's not that hard to do."

That was a disconcerting realization. "I guess. But ..."

"You represented her failure," Harry said. "You exposed the whole thing. That probably outraged her. If it hadn't been for you, she'd have probably gotten away with it. She wanted to punish you. And she probably blamed Cybil for not being able to stop you. So, she decided Cybil had to go as well."

"It's scary to think that there are people like that out there," I said.

"Unfortunately, there are people a lot worse than her."

In a few minutes, Lillian came over and sat down. "Can you imagine," she said. "It's like something out of a movie. Or a book. I think books are better than movies, don't you? I love to read. Young people today don't read. Except my grandson, Jason. He reads. I think he gets it from me. He likes to read that science fiction stuff. He told me he was reading one about a girl warrior robot. They write the craziest things in books ..."

Lillian was busy being Lillian, and I wasn't paying much attention. Instead, as I reflected on the people seated around us in the room, I was reminded of how wonderfully resilient most seniors are. We have learned from long experience that regardless of what happens, life goes on. Life has taught us that we don't have a lot of control over what happens, so we've learned to go with the flow. The events of the last few weeks had saddened us, but we'd get over it, and things would soon be back to normal at Happy Trails Retirement Village.

THE END

All of Glenn's books are available through Amazon
You can see all his titles at:
authorcentral.amazon.com/gp/books